DOUBLE TAKE

Bobbi Bowman

Cover designed by Kindle * Cover Designer Bobbi Bowman
Cover Photo Bobbi Bowman

Bobbi Bowman
Printed in the United States of America

First Printing: 2019
Printed by Pyrofuse

Visit our website: www.pyrofuse.com

ISBN 978-1-7331314-0-7

DEDICATION

To the Deaf community,

for sharing their language and culture.

CONTENTS

Acknowledgements

There are numerous people who encouraged and guided me as this thought experiment became a reality. For years this book stayed in my head as I formed the characters and concepts I wanted to include. It took an enthusiastic group of people on twitter to help me move these ideas from my mind into digital musings on the screen of my computer. I owe these wonderful people, who play with words on twitter using the hashtag #FP (Friday Phrases), such gratitude for generously including me in their tribe.

Additionally, an organization of writers using the hashtag #NaNoWriMo (National Novel Writing Month) pushed me to work on my first manuscript. My husband, Robert Fox, was forever a wonderful sounding board and cheerleader as I talked through scenarios and pondered plot twists. Holly Bowman, my kind-hearted niece, allowed me to use her image on the front cover.

Susan Grennan, ASL teacher, curriculum designer, and writing instructor, is the best editor one could hope for. She tirelessly edited and re-edited the manuscript adding notes of encouragement as well as ideas for improvement. If not for her, the manuscript would still be sitting on my hard drive. My sister, Patti Bowman, blazed the trail by becoming a published author, demonstrating the work ethic it takes to follow your dreams. Lucy MacDonald, mentor and long-time friend, was generous with her time and enthusiasm. I am lucky to be surrounded by family and friends who encouraged me to make this novel a reality. Krin Bowman and Carrie Murphy were my personal cheerleaders as they encouraged me at every step. A very warm thank you to all.

Chapter 1

My vision blurs and I realize that I just read the same sentence twice. Almost two hours on the same chapter and my neck feels as if my bones are surrounded by rust. I look up from my biology textbook and spot two blue eyes looking back at me from across the library. We both drop our gaze. With a slow blush creeping up my neck, I look again.

It's Nate, Noah, Nathan…crap, what is his name?

He-who-has-no-name pretends to be looking for a special book. T-shirt, jeans, tennis shoes…standard college garb. But, instead of a backpack, he sports a messenger bag. That's pretty cool. Looks like it might be covered with some kind of original art. Is he watching me? Am I making a weird expression? People tell me I look mad when I study. I'm not mad; well, most of the time I'm not. It's just my thinking expression.

He catches me looking at him again. Or did I catch him? Nate, Noah, Nathan…yes, definitely Nathan. He's coming over. Oh my gosh, he's coming right towards me. I sit up a little straighter and try to look brave and mysterious. Suddenly he stops, crooks his head, looks quickly around the library, and runs at me. He runs right at me!

Before I can raise my hands he grabs my wrists and pulls me to the floor. Ouch. In the middle of the library? Is he on drugs? His eyes are huge and I can see his chest moving up and down through his T-shirt. His hands are like a vise and I angrily push him with my shoulder and wrench my hands free. I rub my wrists, livid. Never grab a Deaf person's hands! Never. I'm furious and struggle to get up. What is wrong with hearing people!

He tries to grab me again and I start kicking and yelling. All the blood leaves his face. He tries to either calm me down or protect the lower part of his body from being pummeled by my kicks. I don't know which and I don't care. He holds his index finger to his lips to silence me.

I'm so mad I can't even think straight and I want to get away from this crazy guy. But he's not touching me or grabbing at me anymore and looks genuinely scared. Something doesn't add up. I take my eyes off his face and look around. Everyone is under tables, crouched low between the stacks, and under the windows. One girl is crying, her chest moving in a sobbing motion.

I look back at him and mouth, "What's happening?"

He doesn't answer. He just points his index finger to the side and moves his thumb up and down.

Gunfire.

We look into each other's eyes. I know what I see in Nathan's eyes is reflected in my own: disbelief and horror.

What do we do now?

Hundreds of images flash through my brain. Shootings at schools, churches, theatres, parties…it is too much. Has the nightmare come to Tandy, Oregon? What do we do now? I push away the images, calm my breathing.

I start to get up and Nathan makes a move to pull me down again. I hold up my index finger as if to say, give me a moment. I raise my eyes over the table and slide my cell phone off the table and back into my hand. It starts to vibrate and I can tell that his phone is vibrating as well by the way he moves to retrieve it. People around the room are carefully moving to get to their cell phone life lines. We read the same thing.

Campus Wide Alert: Suspected shooter or shooters on Chenoa Tandy campus. Follow lockdown procedure.

I watch one of the librarians go to the front doors like some kind of slow moving zombie and lock the first door and then the second. She turns off the lights to make the library go dark. There's still plenty of light shining in the windows for me to see what's going on. I see another librarian go towards the back, probably to make sure the exits are secure. Everyone seems to be stunned, but not frantic. Only one girl is still crying. Then I remember the huge windows. I see several students crouching below them. I point to my phone and gesture that I want his phone. He is taken aback for a second, then hands over the phone. I type my number into 'contacts' then click on 'text' and hit 'send.' My phone vibrates and I hand him back his phone. He gets it. Communication established.

I type, "Help me get these students from under the window and into the stacks. Bullets might break the glass which would fall on the students and that could be as damaging as a direct hit."

He nods and we move quickly and decisively over to the students, pry them from their area, and direct them to sit down on the floor in the aisles between the stacks. Others, under tables, see what we're doing and crawl to the stacks. I go to the girl who is sobbing. She's talking to me, but there is no way even the best lip reader can understand someone who is sobbing. Where is Franz when I need her? Some Deaf people are just good at lipreading while others are not, no matter how much they practice. Franz is so skilled, she's like a mind reader. But she's not here. I just nod and gently lead the crying student over to the stacks. I sit her down near an older student who gives me a knowing look and a nod. I know the younger student will be in good hands.

"Tell them not to let the lights from their phones be seen from the glass doors at the entrance of the library, even between the stacks.

Tell them to use their bodies to block the light." I type instructions as fast as possible to Nathan.

I could tell he understood because after he started talking, some of the students adjusted their bodies a little.

"You are good," he types. "Have you done this before? I didn't even think of the windows or the glow of the cells."

"I've never been in this situation before, if that's what you mean," I reply. "You take care of the sounds and I'll pay attention to the visual. And Nathan, thanks for trying to get me out of harm's way so fast. Sorry about the kicking. Did I hurt you?"

"Not really," he almost blushes. "Just remind me to never get on your bad side."

Any awkwardness between Nathan and me is gone. We sit, shoulders touching, bending over our phones calling those we care about.

First on the list is Rachel, my sister and best friend. Also my twin. The running joke is that we were roommates in the womb and never stopped. We're different in so many ways, but are fiercely loyal to each other. Once we started high school, Mom and Dad decided we needed a little more room. Dad rolled up his architectural sleeves and created a mini-apartment in our unfinished basement. Before he started there was only a washer, dryer and some 1970's cabinets. Once he finished we each had a room with a bed, desk, chest of drawers, and closet. The rooms are small because outside the room is a big living/gaming area with a small sink, refrigerator, and microwave area in one corner. We also have our own bathroom downstairs. The family laundry room is still downstairs but much updated.

When I went to text her, I saw that she had texted me four times.

"EL, Where are you?" Rachel texts. She uses the letters from my name sign instead of my written name, Elizabeth.

I can just imagine her thumbs flying over the letters on her cell screen, her brow knitted with concern. "I'm in Building 3 downstairs.

I was in the bathroom, for gosh sakes. Someone had to come in to drag me out, bless 'em. I heard the phone buzz with the warning from the college, but I could not…umm…get to my phone at the time. We're secure for now. Most of us are in a windowless room with the teacher's table flipped up in front of the door. This is unreal!

"I'm in the library," I reply, "We're all locked down and most of us are in the stacks."

"It's going to be okay, Sis. I know help is on the way. Stay safe. Love you." Rachel texts.

"Love you right back," I reply. It bothers me to turn my focus away from my sister, but I have more calls to make.

Next comes Franz. That girl could be anywhere. Earlier in the day I saw Franz coming into the library. Petite, thin, big deep brown eyes and beautiful glossy black hair cut in a stacked bob. I would kill for that hair. Dressed in her traditional black, she always looks like she just stepped out of a Goth or Anime film. I've known Franz since we were in the second grade. I call her my second sister. She wasn't carrying books earlier. I remember giving her that "you should be studying" stern look as I pointed to my book and then her. She just smiled, threw up her shoulders in a 'what are you going to do' shrug and followed a cute blonde down an aisle between the stacks. I haven't seen her since.

I send out a text and get an immediate response.

"I got the campus warning by phone and went to the interpreters' office in Building 2. We aren't all here, but we know where the other interpreters and Deaf students are," Franz texts back. "All except Eric. Everyone is secure behind doors. Did Eric text you? I got nothing from him. Glad UR okay."

"I have not heard from him, but he's next on my list," I text back. "Stay safe."

I think Eric has classes today. He missed the deadline for the fall scholarships so he was going to pick up a form for winter. He's been talking about it all week. "You can take an interpreter with you," I suggest. He just rolls his eyes at me. But I know that deep inside he feels vulnerable going into an office and writing out what he needs. I'm sure that's what happened for the fall. But his parents are very upset and tell him if he doesn't even TRY to get a scholarship, he will be finding a job instead of going to school winter term. He is also supposed to see his reading tutor in the Study Skills Center, in Building 2. There are plenty of distractions there as well as food smells wafting up from the Food Station on the main floor. He could have ended up anywhere in that huge building.

I start a text to Eric again when I see another message from Rachel, so I switch over to read her message, "I texted Mom and Dad because I knew they would hear about the campus lockdown. I explained about the protocol and how they would not be allowed in. I also asked them to text Aunt Wendy."

"Thanks, Sis," I text. "Better text Aunt Wendy yourself and tell her no one can get on or off campus. With us in trouble, she'll be in her car and halfway here before Dad finishes the text. I'm making sure Eric is safe. I'll let you know what I find out. Franz is with the interpreters, and I'm here with Nathan – long story, tell you later. Eric has a tutoring session in Building 2 today. Let me know if you get any word from him. I've sent him two messages, but you know about the dead places on campus."

I click send and then gasp at what I've written. The 'dead places' on campus. I can't believe I just typed that. Please let Eric be safe. Please let them all be safe. I met both Franz and Eric in second grade. We've been best friends ever since. I hope he's just out of range. He could be right downstairs from the library and the cell signal would not even reach him. Because of all the electronics, there's something that always goes wrong with phones on the lower floor.

After texting everyone, I lean back against the stacks and just try to breathe. Everyone is accounted for except Eric. What is his schedule? I have a hard enough time remembering my own schedule.

Nathan stopped texting as well and is in the process of checking twitter hashtags that have already started popping up: #ChenoaCC, #WeStandWithTandy #CCC. On the college Facebook page there is a message about the report of gunshots fired. "Multiple shots heard." News coverage is already trying to guess what's happening here. A couple of TV wagons are parked near Paloma Dr., trying to find out what is going on.

The headlines begin floating in my head. As common as these shootings have become, every school, every theatre, every mall, they all say the same thing: "Close knit community. We never thought it would happen to us."

Well, it's happening to us.

My phone vibrates and I hope it's Eric, but I see everyone reaching for their phones at the same time, so it must be something campus-wide.

Chapter 2

Campus Wide Alert: Shooter or Shooters at large. No fatalities or injuries. Security will go classroom to classroom to release students who will be escorted to the parking lot on the North side of the Auditorium. Backpacks may be searched.

No fatalities. I feel as if air is filling my lungs for the first time since Nathan made the sign for 'gun.' Thank goodness, Eric is okay. So we wait.

Nathan and I just sit there for a couple of minutes, phones in our hands, lost in our own little circle of family and friends. I can imagine that everyone across campus is relieved that no one is shot. But could we still be in danger? Is someone just waiting until we let down our guard?

"How long do you think we'll be here?" I pick up my phone and start the conversation by texting Nathan. "If I could get my biology book from over there, we could be studying for the next test."

He read my text and looked at me as if he didn't know if I was kidding or not.

I shrug my shoulders and text "So sue me. I hunger for knowledge." That makes him laugh. I like the way his blue eyes sparkle when he reads my text.

Nathan texts back to me, "No idea how long this whole thing will take. It's a pretty big campus and they say backpacks may be searched. Weird, right? Just to get everyone out and go office to office, classroom to classroom could take longer than I can imagine. Checking out backpacks, that seems crazy."

"I know…maybe they think the person is one of the students or staff and just slipped back in with the panicked students as they started the lock down," I text. "That's pretty chilling. I was so deep into my studies that I would not have noticed if anyone came in at the last minute."

"I was getting ready to study and then I saw you from class, so I just thought…" Nathan's thumbs hesitate over the keys, "…I would come over and see if you wanted to study."

"What did the gunshots sound like? One, or many shots together like an automatic?" I don't have much of a frame of reference, neither parent hunts or shoots for sport or food. The only thing I can imagine is the difference between shots from a hand gun, like in the movies, and from an automatic weapon that sprays the room. Just the thought of bullets spraying the room makes my stomach sink. I have to remember that the alert said everyone is okay.

Nathan thinks about it and responds, "I don't know if I heard the gunshots or the students in the hall yelling about a shooter, but I can remember a little. If I had to say, the shots were close together and there were many of them. It was not like a shot then another shot. Mostly I remember some people screaming about a gunman. That was very clear."

"Thanks again for warning me. I kicked you because one, I thought you had gone crazy, and two, my hands." I lift my cell phone and show him my thumbs on the keys. "Hands are the way I communicate. To grab them like that is like gagging a hearing person. I just wanted you to know."

He looks at me with those blue eyes and nods. "Yeah, I could kick myself. But hey, you did it for me. LOL" he texts. "I'll probably flunk my ASL class for that."

I couldn't help but react. Here's this dreamy guy – who ran across the room to save me, and he's learning American Sign Language. "You're taking ASL? Why?" Please don't let him say it's because it's such a beautiful language or that he wants to date Deaf girls. I've heard both these reasons more than I can count. Not very flattering.

"My whole family is taking it. Well, my mom; younger sister, Emily; and me. We're taking the night class two days a week. My brother, Ben, has been having a hard time and was just diagnosed on the autism spectrum. He's smart and can build and take apart any machine you put in front of him. Okay, he's better at the taking apart than the putting back together. But he is clearly smart. But he can't make himself be understood. So he gets mad…a lot. His doctor thought it would be helpful if we all took sign language so we could teach Ben and he could feel more in control. I want to travel in the future and think it would be cool that I can go anywhere in the world and meet deaf people and sign with them." Nathan texts.

I respond, "I think it's great that your family is learning sign to help stimulate Ben's communication. But one thing, ASL might not help you in other places in the world. Each country has its own sign language. I have a friend in Texas who knows both ASL and Spanish sign language, which are very different. He had to learn them both separately."

Nathan furrows his brow as he reads, "Why are sign languages different?"

I answer, "Why are languages different?"

He reads and thinks about this and nods. "It would be nice if all deaf people signed the same."

I smile back at him, then text, "It would be great if all people signed. Is your dad learning, too?" I asked. The minute those words showed up on his screen I knew I had asked the wrong question. I could see his jaw line tense.

"My dad is a very busy man" he typed, as if with practiced precision. And the conversation stopped there. "What about you? You seem to be calling a lot of people."

"I have a twin sister. We're very close. Our whole family is."

"Is your sister Deaf, too?" Nathan pushed send, then gave me a grimace. He typed "Is that okay to say? Am I out of line?"

I laugh for the first time in hours. Students turn and look my way. I'm sure they are thinking…who could be laughing at a time like this? "No problem. My sister, Rachel, is hearing and I'm Deaf. We were born identical twins, down to the last freckle. However, we were premature. Medical staff put us in separate incubators. Although it was the late 90's not every hospital was digitized. My parents were living in Maryland at the time. There was something wrong with my incubator, and because of an oxygen failure, I became Deaf. It's totally okay to talk about. I don't live my life wishing I was hearing. However, there are many times I wish the world could sign. That would be amazing. So, ASL student, you've been taking the class for three weeks, show me what you got!"

I hit send and watch his expression carefully. Enjoyment and terror…how can that be an expression?

He puts his phone down, turns to me, and starts signing "My name N-a-t-h-a-t. You name what?"

I give him the 'okay' gesture and slowly spell my name. Then I point at him and help him with the difference between the 't' he spelled and the 'n' he meant to spell. We sign back and forth…returning to our phones when there is miscommunication. Different from other beginners, he isn't afraid to throw in gestures and mime when communication begins to break down. I figure that for the last four years he's had a lot of time expressing himself to his brother. Some of the other students join in and time goes by faster than we had anticipated.

After about an hour and a half, Nathan and others turn their heads and move in a way that alerts me that they hear some kind of sound. Nathan gestures a knock on the door. A woman in a police uniform has her badge pressed against the glass entrance. She has access, but wants to let us know who she is before she enters. I can see faces of relief and chatty smiles as we all unbend from our hiding places. She is accompanied by Sara, a campus interpreter (What a sight for sore eyes) as well as a CCC campus security guard. The officer wants us to gather our belongings so that she and other campus security can come to each of us and do a quick search before escorting us to the parking lot. We dutifully stand by our things while they are looked through. I did a mental inventory and was glad there was not something in there that would cause me embarrassment.

But, something didn't seem right. We have all seen enough TV coverage of school shootings to anticipate the process. Students are usually escorted out of the buildings with hands held high or placed on their heads. No backpacks are looked through until later. Safety first. What is going on?

I ask the interpreter, but she either does not know or can't say. Interpreters work by a strict code of ethics where they are forbidden to share information learned in one conversation with those outside that conversation. Because the only reason the interpreter is 'in the room' is because the Deaf person can't hear and the hearing person can't sign…there are strict rules about interpreter conduct. This is very important for the process, but kind of sucks right now when I want more information.

Once our backpacks are inspected, campus security and the police officer give them back to us for the trip to the parking lot. The Chenoa campus is big, but there is enough security to make the inspections go relatively fast. We get to the parking lot and it's filled with students chatting to each other. The first person I see is my sister. I know it's silly, because neither one of us is hurt, but I tear up. We hug each other and our hands start flying as we share our experiences. Nathan moves into the crowd to catch up with the people he knows. Rachel and I see a group of signers and head toward them. I sign very small to Rachel, pointing out Nathan and telling her what he did to save me and how I kicked him. We dissolve into giggles.

Rachel explains how she was downstairs in Building 3 in the bathroom, as she told me in the text. She had just finished using the toilet and was washing her hands when some older student or maybe a teacher with huge, scared eyes came in and said, "Take cover. There's a shooter. Go to a room with a lock."

"I just stood there with my hands dripping with water," Rachel signs. "I was frozen and could not get my brain to work. It was as if I didn't understand the words…shooter, go, lock. The lady looked under all the stall doors then came back to me where I had not moved. She got some paper towels from the dispenser, pushed them in my hands and steered me out of the bathroom into the hall. Something snapped when I saw the rest of the students rushing into rooms. I thanked the lady and took off."

"Did they check your backpack?" I asked her.

Rachel nodded and signed, "All of us."

I see Franz by the other interpreters near Deaf students who are signing and sharing stories. Franz is sputtering. Not much bothers her, so when it does…watch out. She can't find Eric and one of the interpreters is still not there. But, and this is what makes her mad, none of the other interpreters appear worried. When we ask where Matt, the interpreter, is, they just shrug their shoulders and say that the police told them that no one is hurt. Yeah, we get that. No one is hurt. Where are Matt and Eric? Why isn't Eric answering his text?

Even though Franz was born Deaf, she's one of the best lip readers I've ever met. People don't automatically become skilled lip readers just because they happen to be Deaf. As a matter of fact, you either have to have a great grasp of the English language or have a natural talent. For Franz, it is the latter. I use my body to block my signs and ask her if she can read the lips of any of the campus security or police. With a glint in her eye, she starts to scan the crowd, walking innocently around the growing group. She loves this kind of thing, and I usually like to watch Franz work her magic except that I have such a bad feeling about this. Eric still is not here.

Rachel tries to learn anything new about what is going on as well and talks to the hearing students and staff, listening to their experiences. A couple of TV vans pull into the parking lot emblazoned with the stations letters KATU and KOIN. Rachel starts shadowing the crew, not to be on TV, but to pick up any information about what they might already know.

I see her head pop back as if she had been hit. She turns to me and I watch an expression of confusion and disbelief. "There was no shooter," she signs making each hand into a big zero. "And the police took Eric."

Chapter 3

What? They have Eric? Sweet, goofy, fun-loving Eric? Why? "What do you mean?" I ask, which is really stupid. Rachel and I have been signing for 18 years together. I can almost read her mind. But my brain can't take in what she is signing. As soon as I knew both Eric and Matt were gone, I was worried. Something didn't seem right. But I passed it off thinking Matt was probably just interpreting for Eric with the English tutor. No. Matt is interpreting for Eric with the police. The police.

I wave Franz over and share what Rachel overheard. Franz went off. She stomped over to interpreters and said she knew the police had Eric and that Matt was interpreting for him. Before the interpreters could explain about their code of ethics, I interrupt them and sign, "I need an interpreter."

Sara knew what was coming next, nodded and followed me through the crowd to find a police officer. The rest follow me like a big sign language train with me as the engine. I don't care if people stop to watch. I just have to find out. Finally we come upon two police officers to the side of the crowd. "Excuse me, Officers," I begin formally, "I would like to know what is going on. I understand you are holding my friend Eric Morales."

The officers take a second to soak in what is going on. It's a little disorienting to have a person obviously talking to you in sign while a detached voice is talking. You want to look at the person talking, that is ingrained in hearing people. But these police officers have had some good training and focus back to my signing right away. They are also aware that they have an audience.

Out comes the only answer they can give. "I'm sorry Ma'am, we are not allowed to give out any information about an ongoing investigation."

"Ongoing investigation?" I reply. "Eric? You think he's the shooter? He has never shot a gun in his whole life. I've known him since the second grade. He hates guns."

"I'm sorry Ma'am, we are not allowed to give out…" the officer begins

"Unless there was no gun. No shooter," I interrupt.

There it was. A quick look passes between the two officers. So, there was no shooter. But what started the students running and yelling that there was a shooter? How in the world could Eric be involved?

"I'm sorry Ma'am, we are not allowed…" one officer repeats his mantra.

I lift my hand as if to stop the police officer's line. "Understood," I sign, flicking my index finger by my head. "I'll be talking to the press over there to see if they have heard anything."

"I wish you wouldn't," explains one of the officers. "It is really too early to give out…"

"Information in an ongoing investigation. Yes, I know. But are you telling me I don't have a right to talk with the press? I'm forbidden?" I emphasize my point by slapping my 'L' handshape against my left palm emphasizing the sign 'forbidden.'

Both officers sigh at once. "You are not forbidden to talk to the press about Mr. Morales. They can't know any more than we do. By the way, who told you that we're questioning Mr. Morales?"

"You just did." I look at them, each in turn to see if I can glean any more information from them and then take off for the two vans, the signing train in tow.

At the perimeter of the parking lot sit two vans with the crew swarming around them. Strangely, the KOIN van crew is packing it in. They consider this a non-story. Rachel, my sister, moves to that van and tries to gather info while they are loading the van. I watch her making small talk, very casually. My sister is good. She has the eyes of a Deaf person. She nods and laughs and is her charming self. Franz and I are off to the side, pretending to find the nearby parked cars very interesting.

The van pulls out and Rachel returns with what crumbs of information she could scoop up. We gather around as she shares that the news crew confirms that there is no shooter. They said it was a prank, a hoax. They have someone Deaf in custody and some kind of proof. They are joking that he did it to get out of some kind of test.

Sara and Franz have their phones out going through hashtags and reading different posts.

#ChenoaCC no shooter, prank,

#WeStandWithTandy Or rather we sit with Tandy,

#CCC So liberal, can't even find a gun in Oregon

#WeStandWithTandy We know it's scary…to have nothing happen.

Laugh all you want at us, Twitter. Our friend is right now answering questions. I bet he's scared. Wish I could be with him just to let him know he has our support.

I approach the KATU van with Sara and Rachel. The crew is standing around waiting to get an official taping for the 4:00 news. They have all their sound bites from students, and just look bored. It appears that they're waiting around for some official who will have something to say. They hope soon.

A few look up and see Rachel and me walking side by side. I know that look, the double take. While we never wear matching clothes like some twins do, when our long, brown hair is pulled back in a simple scrunchie for school wear, from the neck up we look identical. Even in different clothes, we both have the same body type and stride, like watching two runners moving in perfect rhythm side by side. We have found that this unnerves some who can't keep from staring at us. But maybe today we can use this to our advantage. We've been called 'natural beauties' whatever the heck that means. I guess if you have a nice looking face next to an identical nice looking face somehow "Double the wow" (At least that's the phrase our dad signs. But then he has to say that…I think it's a dad rule.)

"Hello" I greet them through Sara, the interpreter. "My name is Elizabeth Carn and this is my sister Rachel. It appears you are waiting for some kind of announcement. Have you heard if they found the person or persons who pulled the prank today?" I'm trying to be as casual as I can and Rachel lets me take the lead.

A camera person, a young enthusiastic guy, is eager to share. "Head of Security will be out in about 10 to announce the hoax and maybe the name of the guy who did it."

"Really?" I say, innocently and wide eyed. "Wow, they already found him or her?"

"Oh, it's a guy for sure. Something about his backpack." This guy is loving this, chatting up two college gals. "So you're twins, right?"

I nod and keep my eyes from rolling.

"You might even know him, because he's Deaf like you," the camera man continues. "Hey Andrew, we have two Deaf people over here that might know the perp. Want to roll some film?"

Rachel opens her mouth to say that she's not Deaf, but I touch her hand. She gets it right away and just stays quiet. I'm fuming that the camera person calls Eric "the perp" and just assumes both of us are Deaf. But if there is a chance to say something good about Eric and get it out there, I'm willing. No one has verified yet that it is even Eric, but who else could it be? All the other Deaf students have been accounted for.

Channel 2's on-air talent, Andrew Carlson, looks over and raises his eyebrows. He pulls himself from his folding canvas chair and walks over to us. He gives Franz the once over and then takes in the little group.

"Is there an interpreter here?" he asks, as if we were not just recently talking through an interpreter with the camera person. Sara raises her hand. He then continues to talk without even asking if Sara would interpret for him. He just assumes. "Do any of you know a Mr. Eric Morales?" The question lands like a boulder to my stomach. I mean, I guessed it was him but I really didn't want it to be him. We all four raise our hands, like in some grade school. I hate this.

Chapter 4

I begin signing to the on-air talent and Sara voices for me, "Franz and I have gone to school with him since the second grade. My sister, Rachel, has known him that long. Sara, would you like to say how you know Eric?" This is kind of awkward for the interpreter because she has to shift from interpreting to speaking for herself. I give her the lag time she needs. She voices the last of the sentence, shifts her body a little and speaks for herself.

"The term started three weeks ago. I've been interpreting for Deaf students here those three weeks." Sara signs and speaks at the same time, using a combination of English signs and ASL. Not an easy thing to do, but she's a pro.

Three weeks is not much time compared to childhood friends, so on-air talent Carlson shifts his focus back to the three of us. Sara returns to her interpreting role.

"Would you answer some questions for the camera?" Carlson asks.

We nod. He snaps his fingers and camera guy is at the ready.

"This is Andrew Carlson coming to you from the Chenoa Community College campus in Tandy, Oregon after a full campus lockdown. Sources say that the shooter scare is a hoax. The police right now have in custody a person of interest, Eric Morales, who is being questioned about the hoax. There is no official word on if this person saw something or is involved in the hoax. Here's the interesting part. Eric is Deaf. I'm standing here with three of his childhood friends who are willing to answer some questions. Tell me about Eric. Was he happy at CCC?"

"My name is Elizabeth." I begin answering, "I've known Eric for over ten years. He's honest, caring, and fun-loving and would never hurt anyone. He is against guns. His senior year at the State School for the Deaf, he did a whole paper about the gun lobby in the US. He would never do something to put someone at risk." I try to make it short.

Franz is next, "My name is Franz" She uses a big 'z' in the air so the interpreter would use the name 'Franz' instead of her given name 'Francis' which she hates. "I've known Eric for more than half my life. He's like a brother to me. He's a hard worker and was very excited to come here to college. He would never do what they said. Eric, I hope they are captioning this cause I love you," she finishes her signing and flashes the 'I Love You' handshape right towards the camera."

Next my sister starts talking and there's a scramble to move the mic away from the interpreter and to face Rachel. Andrew glares at the camera person for not telling him Rachel was hearing and the camera person just shrugs his shoulders.

"My name is Rachel, and I can only add to what these lifelong friends have said about him. He worked on the State School for the Deaf Haunted House the last three years. It was all about the fun, not about scaring people or making them freak out and cry. He was always careful with children going through the scary parts. It's a myth that Deaf people can't hear anything. It varies. Deaf people can't hear well enough to understand speech. Eric could hear lots of sounds, even some music, but he hated loud sounds like movie gunshots. If he is a person of interest, it is because he saw something and is helping the police. I do not believe he is involved in any hoax himself," Rachel ended.

"So, there you have it. Three of Eric Morales's fan club." He gives us a wink and signals 'cut' to the camera guy.

Fan club? I look over at Franz, who is livid. She balls her fists and leans forward. I get between her and Mr. 'On-Air Talent' and sign low to Franz. "Let him think what he wants. We got information and we supported Eric. Let it go." She relaxes her hands and nods knowing it's probably good counsel not to let him see Eric's friends as hot heads.

We turn to go and see, slowly approaching, the Head of Security along with several members of the college Threat Assessment Team. The Head of Security looks tired, yet determined, with her jaw set. I heard from others that this was the first lockdown on her watch that had not been a drill or staged by the college Threat Assessment Team for training. Franz, a small group of Deaf students, a staff member who is Deaf, and I face Sara (who is looking pretty tired herself). Sara has been interpreting non-stop since 8:30 am and it is almost four. For an interpreter, that's crazy hard. Rachel, who is fluent in ASL and English says that it's not like talking or signing all day. It's more like lecturing on biology and ice skating at the same time all day.

Janet, another great interpreter, was called in sometime in the afternoon. Sara looks relieved when Janet shows up right when the Head of Security is ready to talk. As if by magic, out comes a mobile podium with mic included. It is plugged into wires coming out of the van. There's a short mic test, with someone I didn't notice before tapping on the mic. The Head of Security steps behind the podium, flanked by the TAT members and begins:

"Good afternoon, students, staff, and community members. My name is Dr. Teresa Soto. I am Head of Security for Chenoa Community College. The fine people behind me are Chenoa's Threat Assessment Team. This is the first full campus lockdown since the taskforce was created seven years ago. We have a short announcement to make. Questions will be answered at a later time, once our investigation is concluded." Having finished her introduction, Dr. Soto reads from the folder she holds in her hands.

"11:15 this morning, students heard what sounded like rapid gunfire between the library and the gym. Students alerted students and staff nearby. Several of our hallway safety phones were used as direct lines to the Security Office in Building 2. As soon as security was alerted, our team began to follow campus lockdown protocol. No cars were allowed to enter or leave without being detained. Our own EMT team was alerted. All of this was done in a matter of minutes.

At 12:08, Tandy police officers arrived and began to sweep the campus, starting first in the areas between the library and the gym. One officer smelled gunpowder, and on closer inspection determined that a fuse was attached to a string of fire crackers that were strategically placed between the buildings to cause the strongest echo and still allow for cover.

At that time we determined the event to be a hoax. We believe there is no shooter. Let me repeat, no shooter. We do not know the motive of the person or persons who did this, but it is a very serious matter.

We're talking to a person of interest. Let me make it clear that any staff member or student is considered innocent until proven guilty.

However, if you have any information about the hoax, please phone or text security or use any of the hallway safety phones around campus. You can talk to anyone who answers the phone 24/7. We hope to come to a quick conclusion about this hoax, bringing the person or persons to justice. Thank you very much for your patience. You can gather your things and leave campus. Evening classes will resume at 6:00 pm. This announcement will be texted through the emergency alert system. Thank you."

The on-air talent approaches the TAT members and begins to ask questions. "This is Andrew Carlson at KATU Channel 2. You said you were questioning a person of interest. Is that code for the person you think pulled the hoax?"

"No," replied Dr. Soto. "It is code for person of interest."

"We heard you were going through backpacks instead of having everyone leave the buildings. Did you find something in a backpack that would lead you to the perpetrator of the hoax?"

"I'm not at liberty to comment further than stating that the fireworks found in a student's backpack matches those that appear to be used in the hoax. That is all." She steps away from the podium as well as the journalist and walks away, followed by the TAT.

I tap Rachel's arm to come with, and catch up with Dr. Soto, who is walking away briskly. I nudge my sister and start signing. She knows to voice for me. "Ah…thanks for saying we can go home. One problem. My sister and I have counted around the office and one of the interpreters, Matt Bishop, and our Deaf friend, Eric Morales, are still missing." I was fishing like crazy. "I mean if Matt and Eric are together, they will know that they can come out or go home. But if Eric is on his own, he still might be hiding somewhere."

She stopped and turned towards us and did that – holy cow, they're twins look – and then quickly took hold of herself. "Matt and Eric are together. The police are talking to them."

"Well…if you want to talk with Matt, as an interpreter, you could just talk to him. But if you want to talk to Eric, you need Matt. So if Eric is your person of interest, you have to know that he would not hurt a flea. He would not even scare a flea. He is the sweetest guy you would ever meet." I'm almost crying now and know Rachel is matching my voice by the expression on her face.

The Head of Security briefly looks around as if noting whether the TAT members are otherwise occupied. She puts her fists on her hips and sighs. "Look, if you are a good friend of Eric's, I suggest the next time you see him, convince him to tell us the truth. A hoax is not the worse crime, but the more he lies about it, the deeper in trouble he will be. If he continues to lie, I can't help him."

"Eric is innocent," I sign empathically. "He would never do anything like this."

"Then riddle me this, young lady" she leans in. "Why did he have firecrackers in his backpack that match the ones used to terrify my entire campus?" She turns and storms away.

Chapter 5

I stand there with my mouth open watching Dr. Soto walk away. There are tears in my eyes and I don't know if I'm terrified or angry. Okay, a little of both. I realize I'm reaching out to Rachel. Franz catches up with us and I explain what was just said.

"Bull," Franz said, clearly angry. "No way."

"Someone slipped those firecrackers into his backpack, that's for sure. But was it to frame Eric or just random…was Eric an easy target? You know how he drags his backpack around with zippers all open. It would be easy for anyone to slip in fireworks," I sign. "He's also Hispanic and although most of the students are cool, there are still some who have prejudices. All those 'Zero Tolerance Harassment' posters hanging around campus are there for a reason. They were put up because there is some kind of bullying on campus. It doesn't matter that Eric can't read or write a word of Spanish. It does not matter that he was born in Tandy or is Deaf. He's still Hispanic, so…is a victim of preconceived notions."

"Agreed. At least they say he is a person of interest, not the suspect or alleged suspect," Rachel signs, spelling out the word 'alleged' for strong emphasis.

Franz starts to tear up. In over ten years I have never seen her cry.

"What if they cuffed him? What if they cuffed his hands behind his back? He won't be able to talk. They'll take his voice."

"Don't melt down on me. I don't think they cuff a person of interest. I think they have to charge him with something. Come on. Matt is with him and can advocate for no cuffs. We know Eric didn't do it, so all we need to do is prove it." I realize that is a brazen statement as if we can just solve the mystery, but I know that if Franz falls apart, I will soon be next and Eric needs us. "What we need is a plan. First we need to find out where they are questioning Eric. No one will tell us, but we know Matt has been interpreting for hours. They'll need to call in a replacement. That means we need to shadow Sara, Janet, and Tim, the other campus interpreters. We coordinate with our phones. Okay?" Both Franz and Rachel nod their heads.

I see Tim and Janet walking together and talking. It takes us a while to find Sara, who is talking to a couple of Deaf students who are still hanging around. "Franz, if you take Sara...do you see her there?" I gesture "I'll take Janet and Rachel will take Tim. Are we good?"

We take off to shadow the interpreters.

I'm so upset that I don't notice right away that someone has fallen into step right beside me and my sister. I look over. Nathan. Oh, gosh Nathan. I stop so abruptly both Rachel and Nathan lunge ahead one step and then step back. "Oh...ah...Nathan. This is my sister Rachel. Sorry...we're trying to kind of catch up with those two interpreters." I look at my sister with a 'help me' look on my face.

She beams at Nathan and says "Hi. Are all your friends okay? Well, I guess they would be since it was some kind of a hoax."

We start walking again...me with one eye on the interpreters, one eye on the conversation and praying I don't trip over something on the ground.

"I heard you all talking to the TV crew. You know the guy they are questioning, right?" he asks.

"He didn't do it," I sign. "We're just trying to find him to see that he's okay. We're hoping the interpreters will lead us to him."

"Why not just ask them?" he asks, confused. "I mean they've known this guy for a while too, right?"

"It's not that simple. An interpreter can't talk about private conversations. They would be out of a job at the school and in the community. Imagine I need an interpreter Wednesday night and the interpreter says 'Sorry, I can't work Wednesday night. I'm going to interpret with Nathan at an AA meeting downtown.' That would be a violation of your privacy."

Nathan processes that for a few minutes. "You can't ask the interpreters, so you're going to shadow them." He smiles. "Right?"

"Right" my sister smiles.

"Good luck with your friend," Nathan says and then gives me a wave goodbye as he heads off to meet his friends.

Tim and Janet go back to Building 2, so I guess they are going to the interpreters' office. It is not unusual for us to be going to the interpreters' office as well, so following Tim and Janet does not arouse suspicion. At the entrance, however, Janet pushes open the door to the office while Tim knocks on a non-descript door in the hallway next to the Student Services Center. Rachel and I immediately see that it is the back of the Security Offices. I text Franz to come join us.

We know that if Tim entered, Eric is probably still in there. Franz gets there and we indicate the door Tim entered. After a few minutes Matt exits the same door. He sees the three of us there. His face is drawn and his lips form a deep straight line. He turns his back and goes into the interpreter's office. Rachel and Franz drag chairs from the Student Services room and we settle in.

Not long after, we see Mrs. Morales with Eric's younger sister, Mara, in tow. Well, it's hard to see who is holding up whom. Their faces are stone, but Mrs. Morales looks as if she has been crying. I stand, and see Mrs. Morales mouth "Elizabeth." Mara begins to tear up and there are hugs all around. Mara signs that they're there to pick up Eric.

"What? He can go? Just like that? They figured out he is

innocent?" Rachel spoke and signed at the same time.

"No," Mrs. Morales said, "We're here to take him, but he's still a person of interest, whatever that means. He's not been charged and because he is 17 and not 18 they are handing him over to us, the family. The police haven't formally charged him, so the school hasn't decided what to do. I guess that's the good news. He's not kicked out of school."

"He's innocent!" I signed, so large, I almost hit Franz in the nose.

"Oh baby, I know Eric's innocent. His heart is so big he would never scare anyone. He's been loving Chenoa and working hard in each of his classes. But knowing and proving are two different things." Mrs. Morales explains and Mara interprets.

"Tell him we love him," adds Franz.

Mrs. Morales and Mara knock on the same door. It opens and the room swallows them whole.

We sit back down and don't say much…each of us in our own little world. Feels like we're sitting in the waiting room of a hospital, waiting to see if the patient makes it through…Stop it. Instead of being all morbid, I need to come up with a plan. First, Eric is not charged. So the fireworks are suspect, but they don't have enough evidence. That means they won't kick him out. That gives us enough time to figure out who is framing him. I guess the question we have not been asking is who gains from a hoax? Is someone crazy or mad at the college? Was it a dare? Was it a joke that got out of hand? Is Eric just someone who came along with an unzipped backpack or was he targeted? So many questions. People do all kinds of weird things and we never figure out why. Vandals. Why do they destroy things? What motivates them?

Two large men come quickly down the hall, on a mission. It's Mr. Morales and Eric's older brother, Daniel, looking as if they just came from work, eyes scanning building and room numbers. Franz and I wave and they come towards us. At the same time the security door opens and out comes Mrs. Morales, Mara, and lastly Eric. No cuffs. He's free!

Chapter 6

I wonder if I should go up and grab him or wait until his dad and brother talk with him. Franz flies off her chair and with wild jazz hands (Deaf applause) rushes across the room running smack into him to hug it out. He smiles. It's a tired smile, but it's a smile. He looks over Franz's head and we lock eyes. "You okay?" I ask him.

"No," he replies honestly, "Not at all."

His dad doesn't really sign that much, at least not well enough for a situation like this, but still shows his love. He puts a big hand on Eric's shoulder and looks him right in the eye, nods, then brings him in for a big hug. Rachel reaches for my hand and we look at each other…identical eyes filling with tears. Daniel punches Eric in his arm and spells out 'gangster,' which is really hysterical because Eric is the least gangster person I know.

We each hug Eric and there is a bit of small talk, some in English, some in sign. I have so many questions, but I know he is exhausted. I hold back and let him lead. It's actually Mara who talks and signs at the same time. "Some idiot lit a bunch of firecrackers and people thought it was a shooter like all the other schools. The place went into lockdown. When the cops found the firecrackers all blown up, they decided to check everyone's backpacks. Somehow, and we don't know how, someone, and we don't know who, put firecrackers in Eric's backpack. The police think Eric did it. They don't have anyone else." Mara takes a deep breath and continues. A heck of a lot of maturity for a 15 year old. "Eric is handed over to the family and will be able to continue college until the police close the case. They really wanted him to confess in there so it would be all over, but Eric wouldn't. He didn't do it."

We hug all around again and let them go back home. Eric wiggles his phone and winks at me on his way out. It's his 'talk to ya later' gesture. He smiles, but the sparkle is not in his eyes.

I look at Rachel and Franz and sign. "I'm suddenly hungry! What time is it?" We all three look at our phones…5:30. It's only 5:30?? Are you kidding me? It's only been seven hours. It feels like days since we went on lockdown. Food Station is closed. They just have pizza and coffee open for the night classes.

"Head on down to Sophia's," Franz said, mentioning our favorite Italian restaurant. "I've got to grab my stuff in the interpreters' office. I'll meet you there."

After filling up with our favorite pasta dishes and salad, we start feeling sane again. We talk it all through from beginning to end. I share about Nathan. Franz cracks us up about the cute blonde she was following. With an exaggerated sad face, Franz tells us that the blonde was not only hearing, but also not into girls.

"Such a waste," Franz sighs.

Our laughter is a combination of exhaustion and breaking the stress we have been feeling all day. We hug Franz goodbye as we leave Sophia's. Once home, the look in Mom's and Dad's eyes makes me feel ashamed that we had not texted them more often in the last few hours. Although it is a hoax, all the stressful – what could have been – energy is still floating in the air. They love Eric as well. He and Franz are unofficial members of our family. "We're okay," I say.

"She met a guy!" Rachel signs, knowing this news would make me blush and my parents very interested. "Not everyone can experience a campus lockdown and end up meeting a hottie."

"You really think he's cute?" I ask. "So do I. He's nice too." Suddenly I realize they don't know the story of how we met. So I explain how he grabbed my hands and did a take down and how I kicked him. I tell the story in a comedic manner, but stop when I see my mom's eyes filling with tears. To her, it could have been real. So I quickly switch to Rachel who told about being in the bathroom and someone coming in to get her.

"But I didn't meet anyone," she pouts. This makes us all laugh.

Dad asks about Eric and we're all back to reality. It looks bad because he had the same kind of firecrackers in his bag and it's October, not a usual firecracker time of year. However, it's possible for students to buy firecrackers in July and throw them in a backpack…and then just throw in some books for school…forgetting they still have leftover firecrackers in there. I mean, someone could make a case for that, but Eric was straight with the police. He said he didn't know how they got into his bag. Even knowing Eric didn't do it, I know how lame that sounds.

"Okay, Eric didn't do it," Dad signs. "We start from there and figure out if someone is trying to get him in trouble for whatever reason or just if he is simply a victim of chance. Were you able to talk with him?"

"Not really. His family was there to pick him up. We'll talk tonight." I said.

"Tell Eric we support him," Mom signs before shifting gears. "Okay, anyone want dessert? I can see by your to-go bags from the restaurant, you ordered enough for lunch tomorrow. So how about some cookies?"

"Mom," Rachel and I say together. "What did you put in the cookies?"

"Just a little of this and a little of that," she signs. "Maybe some coconut oil."

"Darn," Rachel said. "I was really looking forward to a big heap of hydrogenated oils." Mom's a nutritionist and we use the word 'hydrogenated' so often to bug her, we have a special sign for it.

Mom gives us both an exaggerated mean face before heading off to get some cookies. She's back in a flash with plates to take downstairs. We say our goodnights, give them both extra-long hugs, and head on down.

Even with all that has happened today, the instructors won't be changing their schedules for us next week. We still have homework. We change and do our evening brushing routines. I remove my hair scrunchie and take a look in the mirror. My curly brown hair falls past my shoulders and needs some major brush work. Once brushed, I reuse the scrunchie to tie my hair into a back bun. My face looks pale and there are bags under my hazel, red-rimmed eyes. "That's what happens when you cry for several hours," I sign to my mirror image. I wash my face and brush my teeth, add a little cream …that's about it. We don't spend a bunch of time on fancy make up. Now soaps, that's another subject. We do like our soaps.

Homework calls, but before I can even think of work, I text Eric.

I feel guilty when I see that he texted me 30 minutes ago. "How are you after all this madness?" I ask him.

"Mom and Dad are really mad that someone did this to me. They think it is because I'm Hispanic. Maybe it's because I'm Deaf. Maybe it's nothing. I tried to rack my brain all day, wondering when someone bumped me or when I put my bag down. Do you know how many times in a day that happens? I'm glad Matt and Tim were there. I know they can't take sides, but if I had to write out the whole thing, my brain would have been fried."

"Can you meet tomorrow?" I ask, "Do you want help with trying to remember where you were? We could talk it out. What do you think? Want to meet with my aunt?"

"So many questions, haha," he writes back. "You know I love your Aunt Wendy, but I think it would be better just to meet with you. About 10, the Cup?"

"You bet. Hang in there." I sign off.

Next I text my Aunt. "Are you caught up on all the craziness at the college?"

"I'm glad everyone is okay, but I'm very worried about Eric. Something like this can follow your record if it is not cleared up," Wendy texts.

"I know. Eric and I are getting together tomorrow to go over what happened today," I explain.

"Ask him if the police made a time line and map. If they didn't, make sure you do. They may just be thinking they already have their hoaxer. Once the college is out of danger, it would not be such a big priority. Connect every place he went today. Something I hate to bring up is that we don't even know how long the firecrackers have been in there. I remember one year he still was finding Halloween candy after Christmas," Wendy warned.

Damn, I hadn't even thought of that. I respond. "One day at a time. We'll just work on today."

"Let me know what you find out and let Eric know he has my full support," Aunt Wendy replies.

"Will do. Love you," I sign off.

I go to our game room and Rachel is there tweeting, draped across the love seat. She looks up. I tell her about my conversations with Eric and Aunt Wendy. We do some negotiation about who gets the car and when it will be back for the other. I'm too exhausted to even think about school work tonight. I then set my alarm, both vibrating and strobe, and turn off the lights and quickly fall asleep.

I feel a slight vibration on by bed. What? Is that my alarm? Is it morning already? I feel as if I have only slept….No, it's my phone. I go to pick up the phone and see the name 'Nathan' and my hand freezes. Wow, he's actually texting me! I check it out.

"Is this the famous member of the Eric Fan Club? I had no idea I shared a library aisle with a famous TV personality. I don't know if I showed the right amount of respect," Nathan types.

I groan, roll my eyes and text back. "I forgot all about the interview. Was it bad? The way 'on-air talent' Carlson behaved himself…he was all flirty and acted as if it was a big joke. I mean it was a hoax, but Eric is in serious trouble."

"You came off looking just fine. I wonder if you want to get together sometime and study for biology or just have a coffee or something?" Nathan asks.

A date? Is he asking me for a date? Maybe he wants to study or just practice his sign language. Hummm. What do I have to lose? "Sure. Biology or coffee or both. See you tomorrow in class." I touch send and flop back in bed.

"See you then," he ends.

Before drifting off to sleep, I suddenly think. What if it has nothing to do with Eric being Deaf or Hispanic. What if it's all about the lockdown? What can be gained from a lockdown? I mean, everything is locked. How can that help anyone? I fall asleep and start dreaming about all the different rooms and how each would be shut down with Nathan and me inside.

Chapter 7

Rachel and I are so in tune with each other, mornings are usually a breeze. But after the stress of yesterday, I need to fly. I love to run and it is good for my body as well as my brain. So I get up about 30 minutes early and clock in a few miles. We have our own bathroom downstairs and while she's a bit messier than I am, Rachel also takes a shorter time to get ready. Neither one of us does more than what my mom calls, 'shower, shave, and shine.' The alliteration means nothing to me, but it means a lot to my sister who hopes to be a great author one day. The one kind of weird thing about our bathroom is the bottles. We love scented shampoos and soaps and can rarely pass a new one up without trying it. Mom tried to keep an eye out for ingredients, but finally just gave up. We have good noses and make sure our purchases don't have a lot of artificial scents, just because we can smell them.

A scented shower refreshes after an early morning run. Once ready for school, I do classwork getting as much as I can done before meeting Eric. We get there about 10. The Saturday morning crowd has thinned out and mostly there are people sitting around with laptops and enormous cups of coffee. I brought a notebook so we can focus. I get a hot tea with a scone while Eric gets a double shot espresso. He looks very tired.

We find a comfortable table for two and begin.

"How are you doing?" I ask Eric, although the bags under his eyes tell me more than any story can.

"Our house is split," he begins. "Mom and Mara think I should stay in school and fight to make the whole thing go away. Dad and Daniel think I should drop out and maybe the whole thing will go away. Then when I come back in a few years all will be forgotten. They don't think I can get a scholarship the way things are and they can't afford to pay for another term. Dad says that there is plenty of work at his shop and that Daniel has been doing a great job and is moving up in the company. Mom and Mara want me to stay in school and do whatever kind of job I want, not just what I can get."

"Wow," I sign, "That seems like you all had a long conversation last night. What do YOU want?"

"What I want is a time machine and for yesterday never to have happened," he signs with angry movements. "Don't think I'm going to get that wish."

I took out my notebook. "I know you are sick to death of answering questions, but if we can map your place and time, maybe that will help."

"I arrived at campus about 8:45 and stopped by the bookstore to see if the 'Chenoa Reads' book was there for class. I put my backpack on those shelves by the door. I know, I know, I should have used the lockers that you feed coins into, but I never did before. I had my wallet and cell on me. Yes, I know anyone could have had easy access to my backpack." Eric puts his head in his hands. I try to express only support. I give his arm a little friendly rub. He continues.

"They didn't have the book, so I went on to pick up some breakfast before class. I went to the Food Station and picked up a few things. It was crowded. And no, I don't remember anyone bumping me or moving my backpack. I ate in one of the cushion chairs with my backpack by my feet. 9:30-10:20 I had math in Building 3 second floor, with Franz. After class I went to pick up my scholarship form upstairs in building 2. The secretary was there. She couldn't find the right papers or other forms – gosh, that place must be a mess."

"10:30 Scholarship Office. Did you put down your backpack?" I ask.

"I don't know. I was pacing back and forth because I didn't want to be late AGAIN with my paperwork. Once she found it she was very helpful showing me the places I needed to sign. Another student came in waiting to be next. We were finally done by 10:50 or so and I went to the tutoring center. The police checked the tutoring center and I had checked-in at 10:50."

"Well, that's proof that you didn't do it! You were being tutored when the fireworks went off. Can't the police see that?" I respond indignantly?

"Sadly, no. Since the interpreter and tutor didn't get there until 11:05 (according to the check-in records), they say I could easily have slipped out, lit the long fuse, and slipped back in again."

"Did anyone see you there the whole time? Did you talk to anyone?" I'm leaning forward signing to him and realize that his face is shutting down. "Oh, I'm so sorry. You were probably asked all this before. But I have a pretty good time line and we can start from there."

"And do what?" Eric asks.

"Prove your innocence!"

"I love you, Elizabeth, but I honestly don't see how. The police questioned me for about two hours, but it felt like ten. They are going to do some CSI crap on the exploded fireworks and see if there are any fingerprints on the firecrackers they found in my backpack. But because no one was hurt, I…I don't know what they will do. I have no record and they can talk to anyone at SSD. I've never done anything like this."

"Since you ARE innocent, there has to be a way to prove it," I say and slam down the notebook (maybe a little too hard since people at the restaurant looked in my direction). " Don't give up. Just keep going to school and keeping your eyes open for something to jog your memory." I finish my pep talk.

"I don't want to go back. Everybody thinks I did it. Look at the Deaf boy, he wants attention." Eric sneers while he signs.

"You send them to Rachel and me," I sign and then put my hands in various fake karate positions. "Or better still. Send them to Franz. She'd take on the biggest bully on campus. But seriously, I know you've been framed. Hang in there. It will turn out okay."

Eric looks down and then back up to me. "Dad said there's a positon open at his furniture shop. I could work there and take some classes online."

"Is that what you want?" I ask, already knowing the answer. "Your brother wanted to work at the furniture shop ever since he could hold a hammer. He's going to have his own design line one day. He's happy at your dad's furniture store and I'm happy for him. But I know you don't want that. You want to be a school counselor or a private counselor. You've always wanted that. Don't be discouraged. Don't let this stop you."

Before he can respond, I show him the time line I'm working on. "Does that seem right?"

Eric nods.

I don't know exactly how to ask this next question. "Ahhh, I know the size of the coffee you drink in the morning. Are you sure you didn't stop someplace else?"

"That's it," he responds, furrowing his brows. "I don't know what you mean."

"Maybe a bathroom??" I ask.

Eric slaps his forehead. "Oh, yeah…Right after math. AND to answer your next question, I didn't leave my backpack 'unattended'," he responds, using air quotes. "I mean, I ah, I can go and still have on my backpack. AND since I know you are going to ask, upstairs Building 3. Wow, Elizabeth, you're more thorough than the police."

"You're welcome" I sign formally and for once I get a smile. That's progress. "Take a look again."

Timeline Friday

8:45 Bookstore – backpack on shelves

9:00 Food Station

9:30 Math Class

10:20 Bathroom Bld. 3

10:30 CCC Foundations – scholarships

10:50 Tutoring Center

?? Police questions – Security Office

Then I wrote down a good news/bad news scenario.

Good news

Eric didn't do it.

Eric does not have a record.

Eric has not done anything like this growing up.

Police have not formally charged him.

College has not kicked him out.

Bad news

Eric has been framed.

Police think it is him.

Since it is a hoax, not a high priority for solving.

If not solved, students/teachers will think he did it.

Eric reads what I have written and nods. We talk some more, making sure all our ideas are captured. I check my phone and see that Rachel needs the car.

"Study hard," I tell Eric, giving him my best parental gaze. I will see you on Monday. I will see you Monday. I will see you Monday." I sign as if I'm hypnotizing him. We laugh more, which is always a good sign.

Chapter 8

The rest of the weekend is a blur of studying, texting with friends, and facetiming with Nathan. Frankly, the facetime is a bust, because he is such a beginner at sign language. But we did get to see each other's rooms. Most of the time we just text, which is fun. Rachel is on the Chenoa tennis team and had a match Sunday afternoon. She won two out of three games, coming home tired and exhilarated. She and I spend time together late Sunday night creating a Monday game plan. We're going to make sure Eric is with someone at all times. Rachel will check with the President or Dean of Students and see if she can get anywhere with the college's video security system. It's supposed to be this big secret, but everybody knows. We don't know where all the cameras are, but it doesn't hurt to ask.

We'll visit each of the places on the list and try to figure out who is there and if any students are bragging about what they did. Often people who cause hoaxes like to get credit for them, which is a way they get caught. Franz is following hashtags on Twitter, Facebook, and Instagram to see if someone saw something that they didn't report, but put on social media.

Franz has math with Eric so they meet early and enter the class together. He feels like all eyes are on him, but that may or may not be the case. I mean, a tall good looking dark-haired male entering a class with a petite goth/Anime super character would get stares in most any situation. After math they take off together.

My biology test is this morning so I have to push everything else from my head until it's over. Nathan gives me a cute little wave as we take our seats and prepare for the test. Good luck pushing everything else from my head now! Good thing the test takes so much focus.

Eric, Franz, and I gather at the Food Station around 11:30 and compare notes on anything we might have learned. Rachel comes in later, wearing a rather smug expression. She went to security and asked about the cameras around campus. They were very tight lipped and would not give her any information. She then talked to a guy named Steve and someone named Dave. She kept pressing them, politely, but one of them said that if she kept asking questions she could be charged with obstructing an ongoing investigation.

Eric puts his head into his hands again. Rachel starts signing, so Franz gives Eric a nudge.

"First, Dave is kinda cute," Rachel begins and everyone at the table does an eye roll. "Well he is. He was all about being very interested in everything I wanted to say."

"Why in the world would a cute guy want to know every little thing you were thinking or doing?" Franz said, batting her eyes at Rachel.

"The other guard, Steve wasn't having any of it. He's the one who brought up the 'obstructing an ongoing investigation'," Rachel says.

"Noooo," Eric says. "Don't do anything to get YOURSELF into problems with the police."

"Don't worry. It is part of our plan," Rachel reassured him. "There is no way they would let me just waltz in and see their tapes. Also, there is no way I can be charged with obstructing an ongoing investigation. I obstructed nothing. I handed over the time line you two worked out on Saturday. This way they will be looking for tapes at the places and times you figured out with Elizabeth on Saturday. I asked to see the tapes for these times. We knew they would say 'no' but now they have the list. I believe they are conscientious enough about their job to look through the camera tapes if they have not already. I talked to people at the bookstore, tutoring, and outside the Foundations' office, which was closed. I had a group of people looking for cameras outside math class for almost 5 minutes. Hope that gets security's attention."

After a short lunch, we escort Eric to his class then get on to our 1:30. No one gives us a second glance. Eric starts to relax. Tuesday, we follow the same procedure with at least one of us being with Eric while he's around campus. Students don't seem to be acting negatively around him. It seems that students feel that if he's around, the police don't think he did it. After two full days of nothing happening, Eric starts feeling like we're babysitting him. Then he gets news from his dad. The police called and said that the fireworks were tested. While they were the same kind of fireworks used in the campus hoax; Eric's fingerprints were not on them. No one's fingerprints were on the fireworks, which means that someone wiped the fingerprints off. No one would wipe off the fingerprints and then carry around the very same fireworks. The police are keeping Eric in the 'person of interest' category. That's good news for Eric, but does not clear his name. Still, Eric can keep going to college.

Rachel and I get home on Monday and have dinner with Mom and Dad. We let them know what is going on. Later we dig into our homework. I'll find out about my biology test tomorrow. I haul up my backpack and remove my math, biology, and reading books. There's a yellow paper, folded like an airplane. Well, that's curious.

Carefully unfolding the paper airplane, I see that it has writing on it. I read the note, drop the paper and yell out in alarm. Rachel runs over from her room and sees that my hands are shaking. I'm looking at the yellow paper on my desk.

She reads the paper and signs, "We need to show the police. We better show Mom and Dad first or they'll kill us for not telling them about it."

We both re-read the note:

**"Stop asking questions.
Your boy is out of the dog house.
If you continue, who knows what could
be slipped into your backpack next. It's just that easy.
Back off."**

Chapter 9

We go upstairs to Mom and Dad who are just relaxing in the living room watching Shark Tank on the TV and laughing. All that stops when they see our expressions. Mom clicks the pause button.

I hand over the note and sign, "I found it in my backpack."

Their eyes get bigger as they read it once, twice, and then the questions spill out. "This is not a hoax. This is scary. You were specifically targeted," Mom says.

"Here's the weird part," I explain. "I had that big biology exam on Monday, so it was Rachel who asked all the questions to security and the bookstore, and tried to find the hidden cameras. Franz and I escorted Eric to his classes today like yesterday, but I didn't ask any questions."

"Looks like a case of mistaken identity. Whoever this is thought YOU were the one who asked those questions yesterday. They must have followed one or the other of you. I just hate that. A target on my daughters' backs. Who would do such a thing?" Dad starts pacing.

"I know…I was shaking for a while, but now I'm just mad. But maybe it means that we're getting close to finding something out. I remember Dr. Soto, Head of Security said if we had any information we should meet with her or others from the Threat Assessment Team. Maybe we can do that before class tomorrow morning." I suggest.

"Want one of us or both to go with you two tomorrow?" they ask, being as supportive as always.

Although we were rattled when we first saw the note, we tell them that we can handle the situation. Armed with the weird note, we feel we have something to offer. We decide to scan it before handing it over to the Head of Security.

*

Wednesday morning we go straight to the security office. We ask for Dr. Soto and are told she will not be in until 10, so we decide to meet her after class. Since we each have two hours of classes, we set an appointment for 11:00 with an interpreter. Although my sister can interpret for me, she wants to participate herself. She asked all the questions at security and in the other places she visited. We're lucky to be able to get an interpreter at the last minute.

I remember when last I saw the Head of Security, she practically sneered in my face. This time, she looks distracted.

"I know you are concerned about Eric," she says. "Didn't he tell you the police are practically dropping the whole thing? After checking for fingerprints there is nothing more that they can do. He is allowed to stay at Chenoa as long as he does not become too much of a distraction. Everyone makes mistakes."

I'm furious, but keep my composure. I show her the note, which she reads and then looks at from a variety of angles.

"You know," she states, "This could have been written by anyone on campus or in Oregon. Are you sure you didn't write it yourself as further proof of your friend's innocence?"

"Very sure." I sign, then just stand there and watch her. Rachel glares at her as well. "We've asked to see the security tapes and have been turned down. Do you wish to take this threat to the police or shall we?" I challenge.

She says that the police had requested all security surveillance info be downloaded for the 24 hours before and during the hoax event.

"We, with our limited funds and personnel, are going through the process now. We will have all the information to the police by the end of the week. I would be willing to hand this over with the surveillance data. It was a hoax, by the way, and the college is up and running again. We do not have a great deal of time to deal with events that no longer are a threat," she responds.

"What about harassment?" my sister says. "Someone put this note in my sister's backpack. That means she was targeted, shadowed, and then the note was slipped in when she was unaware. If you won't take this seriously, we will be talking to the police." My sister almost stomps her foot; bless her, she is so angry. However, Soto is not at all moved.

"You'll find the police can do little with a note like this," she said, letting the paper float down to her desk. "Were you confronted by someone in the halls? Do you know who put this in your backpack? Could one of your friends be playing a prank on you? Without more proof, sadly, there is nothing we can do. I'm sorry," she says with an expression that does not seem sorry at all.

Rachel and I leave the Security office very frustrated. Do we go to the police? Is someone still watching us? How creepy is that? Do we tell Eric? Rachel thinks we should because it is part of the whole mystery he is involved in. I'm not so sure. I saw the look on his face when he talked about not coming back to Chenoa. If he thinks we're in danger, I don't know what he'll do.

We go to the interpreters' office and see if Eric and Franz are there to pick up a bit of lunch. We catch them up on what happened and show them a copy of the paper. Franz, of course is livid. Eric is just overwhelmed. We pick the note apart line by line wondering the writer's intent. Will there be another hoax? Will he or she place drugs in there and then turn us in? I have no idea.

Franz says, "I think the Head of Security is wrong about the note. It is harassment, and I think you can call it that; because it is a threat, you can talk to the police. This happened to a friend of mine last summer. She got these really bad hate letters about being a lesbian. Since sexual orientation is a protected class, the police could take a look at it."

"Although the letter was intended for Rachel, the hoaxer put it in my backpack because he or she got us mixed up. So is this a 'protected class' situation?" I ask. After thinking it through, I decide that we need to take it outside the college.

I ask Rachel, "Can you go to the police station after the your last class? Mine ends at 3:00 pm."

She says she could. Frankly I don't have much of an appetite for lunch or my math class (although I like both of them just fine). I keep looking over my shoulder wondering if anyone is shadowing me.

After class Rachel and I head out to the police station in downtown Tandy. Of course it happens again. As soon as we walk into the waiting area, everyone does a double take. They try not to, but just cannot help themselves. We pretend not to notice.

Since we're not on fire, and are not here to talk about a violent crime, we have a lot of waiting to do. Rachel takes out a book and starts reading. I think if my sister tries to go for more than 15 minutes without a book in her hand something very bad will happen to all of us. I smile to myself. I'm very proud of my sister and her goals. She's taking writing and literature almost every term this year. She's kept a journal since she was able to learn the alphabet. Once when she was 12, I got into her journals. We had the biggest fight. It was, as my parents called it, epic. We refused to talk with each other for almost a week. Writing, as well as reading, is almost sacred to Rachel.

I whip out my phone and make sure I'm up on twitter and FB. I also check out hashtags, some suggesting Eric should not be allowed to stay at the college. Hello people. Have you not heard about innocent until proven guilty? I don't respond because twitter wars never help and always make both sides look foolish.

The officer comes out from behind the door and calls our names. We go back to a private area, I think where they question people. We ask him how much he knows about what happened at Chenoa Community College last Friday. He is up to speed so we tell him about going to all the different places, looking around, and even asking to view the security tapes. We get an eyebrow lift from the last statement.

Finally we get to the note that was put in my bag Monday during the day telling me to back off. We also share how we think the hoaxer mixed up my sister and me. She was the one asking all the questions on Monday, but I got the note in my backpack. We then say that we handed over the note to the Head of Security at Chenoa this morning, but she thought not much could be done. I've got to hand it to the officer, he didn't dismiss us but waited patiently throughout the entire time we explained.

"Your friend, Eric, remains a person of interest," he begins, "But we don't have enough to hold him. However the event is not closed. He is able to continue college at Chenoa. That's the good news. The bad news is this note does not really help his case. With the fireworks and even this note, no one was really hurt. We have no way to know who put the note into the backpack, or their intent."

"Can't you have someone read the note and tell if it was a male or female and maybe 'profile' the person?" Rachel asked.

He presses his lips together and I know he is stifling a grin. "I think you have been watching a little too much CSI. So much of that stuff is not even real. It is not a violent crime and we don't have the resources to bring in the CSI team. I don't mean to put you down, but there was a couple shot in NE Tandy last night and a string of burglaries nearby. Our hands are full, and as the note says, your friend is 'out of the doghouse.' I suggest you just let it go."

We thanked the police officer, but left the place dejected. What now? I hate the idea of giving up and just letting Eric stay in this 'person of interest' limbo. If anything happens at the college, he'll be the first one they talk to because of the frame job.

Rachel shakes her head as if having an internal dialogue with herself. She begins to sign, "I don't like how Dr. Soto dismissed the note. I wonder if we should share the same information with the other members of the Threat Assessment Team.

I also don't like that the security info has not been sent to the police yet. I mean, sure, it is not the top priority, but a bunch of security people were there. Not the night crew, of course, but why would it take so many to download the cameras? How many cameras are there?"

Good questions, all, I think, then laugh out loud. Rachel gives me a funny look as if the pressure is getting to me. "Good questions, all," I sign. Rachel's expression goes from confused to a full tooth grin.

Chapter 10

Aunt Wendy. Every time we had a problem we wanted to talk out, we'd go to Aunt Wendy. One of the really wonderful things about her is that she never fixes anything. She rarely gives advice. She just listens. Really listens. Her favorite phrase was "Good questions, all." We would talk until we had figured out our next step. She'd smile at us and do the Deaf applause, shaking her raised hands back and forth.

"Maybe we should visit Aunt Wendy," we laugh, Rachel starting the sentence and me finishing it as we do so many times. I bet she's getting ready to leave for the day. Maybe we can catch her before she leaves. We text and she says come by the Deaf School library.

We drive by Dutch Brothers and pick up Aunt Wendy's favorite, along with mochas for ourselves. "Beware nieces bearing gifts," Rachel teases. We arrive at the State School for the Deaf and go around to the library by the track. I ran many a mile on that track all through my schooling.

The doors are locked because the school day is over for the kids. We stand outside while I text Aunt Wendy to come let us in. She comes to the door and does a mock double take at the third coffee we hold up.

"Yummmm" she fingerspells, making the 'm' flutter. "My favorite nieces have come for a visit and brought me a treasure. Thank you kindly. Your dad tells me you are having some excitement over at the college. How are you two? And how is Eric holding up?"

We gathered around one of the tables and made ourselves comfortable. We catch her up on what Dad hasn't told her. She listens and sips her coffee, nodding her head or making the 'y-handshape' nod with her hand.

"One of the things I worry about most is Eric dropping out after working so hard to get to Chenoa. You know he will be the first in his family to attend college? They are so proud of him, but he feels a cloud hanging over his head as he walks the halls. Franz, Rachel, and I escorted him to his classes the first two days, but he won't let us babysit him for long. He's got his pride," I explain. "But Monday night I found this little gem in my backpack." I show Aunt Wendy a copy of my note. Both of Aunt Wendy's eyebrows fly up and she shifts from a listening position to one of worry. Then I share about going to Dr. Soto and what was said.

"Do your mom and dad know about this?" she asks.

We nod our heads. We shared about our trip to the police station and what they are and are not willing to do to help clear Eric.

"They didn't even seem concerned about me," I share. "They didn't ask for a copy of the note or anything. I guess they'll get the original when all the data is transferred to and copied on a memory stick for the police. Dr. Soto thought it might take a while to find exactly the right time indicators and copy everything for the police. Chenoa does not have the latest security systems. The system can't even be viewed from off site.

Aunt Wendy chuckles and rolls her eyes. "I know that feeling. We have some of the cheapest security systems covering some of the most expensive equipment. Crazy, but that's how finances are sometimes when voted on by a committee." She looks at them and says, "Well, girls, what's next?"

We shrug as one and Aunt Wendy smiles.

"Okay, what's top on your list?"

"My biology test results," I laugh. "See if Dave is single" Rachel adds. We all start laughing and it feels really good just to laugh. For a few seconds we just smile and sip our coffee.

"Seriously, I don't want Eric to quit. How can I get him to stay? We don't know if he was targeted, but we sure know Rachel or I were. How can we help the process along? Do we go to the press? Do we try to raise money for a reward?"

Aunt Wendy is nodding, "Good questions, all."

Rachel and I dissolve into giggles and our aunt looks from one to the other and slowly raises her eyebrows.

"Sorry," Rachel said. "But we knew you were going to say that."

"Yuck" signs our aunt, "I hate being that predictable. While I don't usually give advice, I have some suggestions. Number 1: Eric missed his first scholarship deadline, which means that he may have been a little torn about going to college. Don't let him miss the next deadline. Help him fill out the papers so he can't say that he missed the deadline again. Number 2: Stop babysitting Eric. When YOU have moved past this, then he will be able to also. And lastly, Number 3: Zip up your dang backpacks!"

We all start laughing again. After giving her hugs, we head home for dinner and study time.

I catch up with Franz first, texting her what has happened with Aunt Wendy. Of course she bemoans that we went without her, since everyone who's ever gone to SSD loves Aunt Wendy. Very few outside of the family can call her Aunt Wendy, and two of those are Eric and Franz.

Eric is glad I volunteered to help him fill out his scholarship pages. I have to do mine, too, so it will be easier to do it together, with my sister (the English wiz) on speed dial.

I send a casual text to Nathan about my day and realize that I never told him about the note. I'll see him in the morning for biology (argggg and to get our test results). Once all the texts are sent out, I sit at my desk and do some homework. This hoax thing has really been eating into my study time. But maybe it will work out.

It finally looks as if we can all move on. However, deep inside I really don't like the idea of a stranger telling me to back off. If it is really a hoax, why would someone risk doing that?

Chapter 11

It's Wednesday morning and Nathan is not here yet. I'm sitting in biology waiting to turn over my test and see the score. I think I did a pretty good job on it, but you never know. I flip the test over. 'B' 87%. Okay, better than a 'C,' but I have to do better. Being a veterinarian is all about the sciences. I'm great with animals, all kinds. Mice to elephants, alligators to sloths, bring it on. Okay, full disclosure, I have never worked on most of those animals, but I'm willing to learn. While a 'B' is good, I'm going to have to raise my grades. Maybe if my best friend is not charged with locking down the whole school, I can study more. No, no excuses.

Nathan comes in and takes the chair next to me and exhales, just as I did, before turning his test over. He got an 'A' 91%. I smile to myself. I always like them smart. I show him my grade and he gives me a thumbs up. I go over the syllabus to see if there is anything about extra credit. YES! There is a list of activities I can do. I read through which ones will put me in the 'A' category and what I might be able to do for future tests. The extra credit looks hard. I star a couple I think will help me.

We begin the class and I'm right there, watching the interpreter, soaking in the information. I have a note-taker, actually two. I can't watch the interpreter and take notes at the same time. My eyes would have to split. Most Deaf students have one note-taker. Either another student takes notes on a type of carbonless paper offered them by the Student Accessibility Office, or the student takes notes on a laptop or tablet then emails me a copy. For biology, the foundation of my studies, I ask for two volunteers. This way I combine their notes with notes I take from the textbook. Everything is then put together to make what Rachel calls mega-notes. I try not to miss anything. The process of combining the notes with the information in the book helps me study. My result is a great blue-print for future study. I'm not taking this class to get through it, I'm taking it to 'get it, own it.'

When class is over Nathan and I sign a little, but we quickly move to texting. While he's doing well in his sign language class, his vocabulary is very limited. I tell him about the note that was slipped into my backpack and he wants to read it, of course. I pass him the copy. He reads it and gives me this…'what the heck?' look. I catch him up on the Head of Security's response to the note.

"S doesn't seem concerned about the note. She acts like the NOTE is a hoax. Why doesn't S take this seriously?" I type quickly, showing my frustration.

Nathan reads the text, then looks puzzled. "Who is S" he types.

I have to read over my text to understand what is confusing. "Sorry, I typed 'S' instead of 'Dr. Soto' because I was in a rush and in my head I was thinking of her name sign instead of spelling out her whole name." I type. He still looks puzzled so I explain further. "A name sign is like short-hand for a person or a place. I use S for Soto and use the sign placement for 'police' for Head of Security. Instead of spelling out D-R-S-O-T-O-H-E-A-D-O-F-S-E-C-U-R-I-T-Y, I use S." I show him the sign.

"Wow, that does save time," Nathan nods then texts back. "I want to learn more of those."

"In time," I smile at him, liking his positive energy.

I also share our more positive encounter at the police station and later my visit with Aunt Wendy. When I get to the part about zipping up my backpack he looks over and sees at least two pockets unzipped. For that, I get a look that makes me giggle. He lowers his head just a little and one eyebrow arches. Adorable. And, he's probably done this before to other females who consider him adorable.

"Want to grab some pizza this Friday at 6?" he texts.

"Sure" I reply, trying to keep my thumbs from missing keys. Auto-correct, don't do anything crazy, okay? "Want to meet at the pizza place or what?" I leave the question up in the air.

"I'll come by and pick you up at 6. Is that okay?" he asks.

Okay? Yes, okay. That means this is a real date! I have to be cool. I type him my address and we exit the classroom as the next class enters.

In the afternoon, after math, I have reading class. It is tough, but I have Sara as the interpreter. I like her style of signing, as clear as skywriting. Also, I take the class with Franz, which is always nice. As is common practice, we sit in front of the class so there is little distraction between us and the interpreter and instructor. This also gives interpreters a direct line of site as they need a clear view of our signing as we participate in the class. Being the only Deaf person at the front of the class is logical, but not as fun as having casual social interactions like the hearing students do in class. In light of recent events, knowing there might be someone behind me ready to slip something in my backpack creeps me out. Sara is a 'by the book' interpreter when it comes to the code of ethics, so Franz and I know she will not only sign what other students nearby are saying, but she will also voice what Franz and I sign to each other. We learned that the hard way the very first week.

Eric finishes his reading class the same time Franz and I finish ours. I go to meet Eric upstairs in the Study Skills Center right next to Tutoring. I float each time I remember I have a date with Nathan. A 'B' in Biology and a weekend date with Nathan…and only the fourth week of the term.

Eric already has a table for us with his scholarship paperwork out. I pull mine out and we begin. About half way through we're signing and arguing over what a certain line stands for. We're like siblings. It means this, no, it means that. I put the papers side by side and see that Eric has the wrong papers.

"Is this what you got from last term that you never handed in?" I ask.

"No, this is what I got last Friday at the Foundation's office," he responds.

I show him where the date is wrong on his paperwork. It says 2018. That's for this term. You need the 2019 form. "Didn't you say the lady at the front desk had a hard time finding the right paperwork? Well, she never did. She gave you the wrong papers."

"No, she looked at them carefully. See the 'X' here and here," Eric shows me the places where the secretary had shown him were to sign.

"That doesn't even make sense," I tell him, "This is where your counselor signs her name."

"Enough!" Eric uses the sign for 'finish.' "Let's just ask her. Should we get an interpreter?"

"Nahh, we can just write back and forth."

We exit the Study Skills Center and head over to the Foundation office. The lights are on inside but the door is locked. I look down at my phone's clock. 11:00 AM. It's not lunch. On the door is a small sign:

Foundation Team Conference – Washington State

Office closed: Friday, 10/16 – Thursday 10/22

If you have questions, please contact the Counseling Department

*

What? Closed last Friday? Closed when Eric picked up the wrong form? What is going on?

"Did you say that the secretary had a hard time finding the scholarship form and the place looked messy?" I'm looking at Eric. He just nods. What is going on here?

"Wait a minute...," I sign to Eric, then cut off mid-sentence. "I remember now. Rachel said the office was closed on Monday. She didn't say it was closed from Friday on...that just does not seem right."

"I'm going to the security office to talk to the officers. This is just crazy." Eric turns to go.

I stop him and say, "Maybe we should not ask the officers just yet. I mean, why didn't they know the Foundation team was at an off campus site? They are security and should know all that."

Eric is frustrated again. "I was with the police when they asked me specifically where I went that day. They were the ones who knew my schedule. Campus security was doing other things. They didn't know I went there."

Something is starting to form in the back of my brain. "They didn't know you went to the Foundation Office until Rachel gave them the list on Monday. It was Monday I got the note in my backpack." I text Franz and Rachel where we are and to come STAT.

"But why? Why lock down a whole school?" Eric asks.

"I'm thinking it has something to do with this office and the person who was there. Person or persons. You said someone else came in while you were there. While she helped you with the paper, putting the 'X's' in the wrong place, by the way, was he there too? Did he seem interested? Was he leaning over?"

"Last Friday, today is Wednesday. Hummm, how can I say this... I don't remember!" he smacks his head and starts pacing.

Eric is sputtering his hands around, half signing to himself. After a few minutes he just seems dejected, shoulders slumping and hands still. Franz and then Rachel come, worried expressions on their faces. I point to the sign taped on the door. So they were all gone Friday. ALL gone.

"We came here to clarify something because a lady gave him the wrong packet and marked for him to sign in the wrong place." I explain. "If the place was closed, where was the sign and why was the lady there? Why hadn't she just said she was trying to find something and Eric should go to counseling?"

In my imagination, I could see my Aunt Wendy signing, "Good questions, all."

Rachel asks, "Why the Foundations office? I know they give scholarships, but what else do they do?"

Franz knows this one. "Ask for money. All the time. My parents are always talking about how they get an email or postcard for fundraising every other month. They ask for money from students, staff, alumni, parents and family of students, and community members. It's a big deal. Between the four of us, three are requesting scholarships."

I wonder if the money is separate from the college money.

Rachel signs, "Look, here's Steve from security. I thought you didn't call security yet?"

I watch a uniformed guard coming quickly towards the four of us.

"I didn't" I sign, hit 911 on my phone, and slip it in my purse.

"Is that security?" Eric signs. "I think that's the guy who was waiting for the scholarship packet."

Chapter 12

"I want to thank you clever children for standing right in front of the security camera to have your little meeting." Steve sneers and moves past us and opens the door to the Foundation. "Should you have left this little school lockdown excitement as a hoax? Yes. Don't you smart college types have homework to do instead of putting your nose into other people's business? I think you do."

Rachel, on automatic, interprets what Steve is saying.

"Well, you kinda made it my business when you framed me for the firecracker stunt." Eric signs as he positions himself between us and Steve. Franz and I exchange surprised expressions. Was Eric bluffing?

"Are we sorry about that? Yes we are." The security guard over-exaggerates his lip movements and rubs one eye with a fist gesturing fake tears. "So that is why we decided to show you what we've learned." He gestures for us to enter the Foundation's office and we slowly file in. Once in, he stands with his back to the door. "Here's what we've learned. Are you as gullible as a puppy? Yes, you are. Sign it, interpreter girl. Don't miss any of it," he looks over to Rachel.

We bristle and Franz steps towards him. "There are four of us and one of you." She holds up the number four near her chest to symbolize the four of us, and on the left hand, closer to him, she has the number 1. But she chooses to use the middle finger instead of the index finger to symbolize number 1.

"Nice one," he mocks, "Did I bring a friend? Yes. Yes, I did." He pulls a gun out of his jacket pocket.

"Security guards can't carry guns on campus," Rachel says. While her face looks calm, I can see the tremor in her hands.

"Well, you see, I'm not a very good security guard," Steve mocks. "Now, that I have your attention, let's go a little farther in."

The Foundation Office is larger than it looks from the outside. The front area is more like a greeting area. Then there's a short hall with four offices, two on each side. Each office has a solid wooden door and then a window going from the ceiling to half way down the wall. He moves us to a middle office where he has us drop all our backpacks, purses, wallets, ID's, everything except the clothes we have on our backs. He pats each of us down for any smart watches, fitbits, or anything that we could possibly hack to call out. This is not good. He has enough training to know what to look for. One by one we are zip-tied, while Rachel continues to interpret.

Steve Wallace (according to his name tag) lets us know that we're his insurance, and that while he has not hurt anyone yet, he is willing to 'get a little bloody' if we don't behave. He has a partner who is sitting outside the office for the next hour pretending to study. He is very clear, "If my partner hears a peep before that, he is to call me immediately. I will return with my silencer. Why, yes I will. Once I tie up a couple of details, my partner and I will be on our way. Will someone come before you all die of hunger?" He looks at each of us then shrugs dramatically.

Wallace then leads us to the back office. Rachel's hands are zipped tight. He turns off the light to the office and locks us in. He gives us a little wicked smile through the office side window where some light is still streaming in and we know what will happen next. He'll turn off the lights to the whole Foundation Office and we will be thrown into complete darkness.

I can't see, I can't hear and I'm near panic. This is my nightmare, that I see the outside world. My breathing is jagged, and the darkness is messing with my balance. I jump when I feel someone's butt scooting into mine. What the hell? I can't even think straight.

It's Rachel. She grabs my hands and I cling to her. She spells "Ok, ok, ok, ok, ok" into my hands until I calm down. "Remember our game?" she spells the letters into my hand and finishes with a question mark drawn into my palm.

I make a fist and nod it up and down like a 'yes.' When we were young, our first hero was a famous Deaf and blind woman by the name of Hellen Keller. We read her story again and again. At night after we were told to stop giggling and the light was dimmed, we would sneak into each other's beds and play Hellen Keller.

"We're safe." Rachel spells, "This is an office. We can find something in the office to cut the ties. Help me look, ok?"

"Yes," my fist nods.

We back up to the desk and start moving things around. Suddenly the lights blink on and there is Franz, our tiny personal ninja. She had stepped through the zip-tie and once her hands were in front, moved around until she could find the light switch near the door.

"Now, ladies and gentleman," she signs clearly even with zip-ties on, "Let's get the heck out of here!"

We start opening and closing drawers in earnest, looking like a comedy sketch doing everything backwards, except for our Franz. Dang, Wallace must have grabbed the scissors on the way out. No sharp letter opener. Wish the office had one of those staple removers. That would work.

We keep looking, but our spirits have lifted, knowing that there is no gun in our faces. Eric finds a key chain way at the bottom of the lower drawer. There are the most beautiful-looking nail clippers hanging from the key chain. Jackpot!

Franz begins and soon we're all zip-tie free, rubbing our wrists and trying to calm the adrenalin rush running through our bodies.

Step 1, accomplished. Step 2, now to get out of the office. Eric and I both put our shoulders against the door, but it stays firm. We look around for something we can use to break the narrow strip of window that is to the left of each door in the inner offices.

"Wait," Rachel says. "That Steve guy told us that he had someone sitting outside in the study area for the next hour. Won't that person hear the glass break and call him?"

"Well, he also said that we were 'gullible as a puppy' so I'm thinking there is no friend outside. I would bet Steve and that fake Foundations woman split." I counter. "But I think we should all have a say. I mean, if I'm wrong, Steve may be willing to do some damage to keep his secret safe so they can escape."

I look to Eric. "Break it," he says.

"Franz?" I ask.

"You know what I'm going to say. I'm ready to break a little glass." Franz replies, spelling 'glass' instead of using the sign so she can emphasize the a-s-s part of it.

"Okay," Rachel says, "We're all in. But let's decide right now our next moves so we don't just cause a bunch of noise and stand around deciding what to do next.

"When I saw the security guard come down the hall, I hit 911 on my phone and slipped it in my purse." I inform them. "I think police have to check on phones even if it seems like a butt dial and no one answers. As soon as we get out, I think we should all call 911 and tell them what is going on. Steve is part of security, so I don't know who we can trust in the security office. I think we should call the police and wait for them to get here."

"I like everything except the staying here part. Once we have called the police, I think we should go to the Tutoring Center right outside and just stay with all those people until the police arrive. On the off chance that Steve comes back, he'll have to do what he threatened to do in front of a whole lot of witnesses," Eric says.

We all agree and start looking around for something with which to smash the window. On the shelves are some impressive looking trophies. But when we pick them up, they are light, made out of some kind of plastic. The chair, we could use one of the legs of the chair, if two of us charge holding the leg like a spear.

"Look at this," I say. "It's a lamp with a metal base, which is really heavy." I take off my jacket and wrap it around my arm to protect it, turn my face, then slam the base against the glass. Weird. I thought the whole thing would come down like in the movies. I made a little hole. So I kept at it until there was a big enough space to put my arm through. My arm is not long enough.

Eric steps in and threads his long arm through the broken glass to unlock the door. Step two accomplished. We all scamper out and grab our gear in the office where Steve stashed our stuff. We each hit 911 as we walk from the Foundation offices across to the Tutoring Center. Three of us are on texts while Rachel uses voice. We're in our own little world for a minute, making the call, answering questions. It takes longer for us than for Rachel, who uses voice. But we all get through. We tell them that we'll be in the Tutoring Center upstairs in Building 2. We warn them about the Security Guard's threat about someone watching us and informing back. The police tell us to sit tight in the Tutoring Center and they will be there.

Rachel also adds that they need to bring someone who is good at computer fraud, because she suspects the Foundation's money has been compromised.

We spill into the Tutoring Center glad it is full of students. We stand by the front counter, a circle of triumph mixed with nervous energy. If Wallace has a friend waiting outside the Foundation Office, that friend probably left as soon as the glass broke. Rachel says it was surprisingly loud.

Chapter 13

Rachel calls Mom and Dad to briefly explain everything that happened. I contact Aunt Wendy and share briefly so, if she gets word of anything on campus, she won't worry. I contact Nathan and do the same. It feels a little weird to call him, since he's not my boyfriend…and it's just been five days since we first texted between the stacks in the library. But he's one of the few people who knows what's going on.

Eric appears curious about this Nathan I'm calling and what he has to do with everything. I tell him that he's the one in the library who threw me down when he heard that there was a shooter. He knew I could not hear the shots and was attempting to protect me.

"…and they have a hot date this Friday night," Franz says, an impish grin on her face.

"I don't think you should be dating anyone while this is going on. We don't know who to trust," Eric replies.

"We were locked in the library together. He never slipped out to do anything. Also, you mentioned a woman and a man. We already know Steve is the man, so the other person is a woman. Nathan is defiantly not a woman," I reply.

"By your logic, I can't even date Dave because he was working with Steve. It's not Dave's fault that Steve is a snake. Please let me date Dave. Please." Rachel is feeling the relief in all this and enjoying being able to tease Eric, who is not amused. The tension in the air is still pretty thick, even with Rachel making jokes.

Once everyone has been called, we don't really know what to do with ourselves. We know Steve the Security Guard is involved, but we don't know who the woman is or if there are any others. We imagine someone is trying to take the money from the Foundation since it is not specifically tied to the college's main fund. Really, we're just guessing because we don't know how the college handles money. We just know that they were doing something in offices that were supposed to be closed.

Rachel waves her hand in a way that gets our attention. She puts her finger to her ear and makes the sign of a flashing light followed by the sign for police, letting us know she hears sirens. Since the lockdown happened only five days ago, students (as well as staff) in the tutoring center are diving for their cell phones once they hear the sirens getting closer. But there is no college-wide alert.

Not long after, four officers come down the hall in Building 2 with a frustrated Head of Security as well as the entire Threat Assessment Team. I'm sure she is humiliated that one of her employees is suspected of a campus crime. She does NOT look glad to see us. She probably has had to admit to the Threat Assessment Team that she did not take the threatening note placed in my backpack seriously. The troublemaking twins and their Deaf sidekicks strike again. They also have two of the college interpreters in tow, Sara and Matt. Well, someone did something right.

Matt starts interpreting for us as we show them the room where we were held, the zip-ties on the floor, and the broken glass. Before we even finish showing them the room, they begin separating us. It feels as if we're the suspects, but I know they have to follow a certain protocol with these kinds of calls. I mean, they still believe Eric is the one who created the first hoax. And now, here he is again, surrounded by his fan club saying something else is going on.

Since there are only two interpreters, and they aren't going to let Rachel interpret for me, I just have to wait until it's my turn. There are four inner offices in the larger Foundation Office, three of which have no glass debris. Three of the officers take Rachel, Franz, and Eric into the rooms. Dr. Soto paces and gets on her phone from time to time, but I have no clue what she is saying.

Five minutes later two people come with staff badges around their necks and keys on their jeans. I suspect that they are campus custodians when I see they have a roller trash can with them. They put on special gloves before Duct taping the jagged hole in the glass so nothing more can break. Then, Duct tape is used to tape 'X' marks all the way from the break to the ceiling. Duct tape is reversed to pick up the tinier fragments of glass that are in the carpet. Then comes the vacuum. Once accomplished, they nod and say something to Dr. Soto who appears to thank them. It is the first time I have been around her when she smiled.

My phone starts buzzing. Aunt Wendy and Nathan are both texting. I raise my phone to Dr. Soto with a questioning look. She nods and I'm relieved that she lets me use the phone. Aunt Wendy wants to know if we need anything and to let me know that she loves me. Nathan says he just read on Twitter that something was going down at the college, and he wonders if I'm 'in the thick of things.' I smile at that.

"Yup," I respond.

"I'm coming to campus," he types. It was not a question.

"I'm okay; the police are here."

"I don't care," he responds. "I'm coming there anyway. I'll be there in 10 minutes."

I must admit, my heart melts a little.

"See you in 10," I tell him. "If they move us, I'll let you know if I can."

"See you in 10," he types back.

I see Franz come out of one of the offices, she makes a two handed sign which loosely translated means, 'no biggie.' The officer waves me in. Here I have done NOTHING wrong (okay, other than wreck an office and break a window), and I feel like I'm going in for a root canal.

I go into the room and Sara is there. The officer begins by showing me a picture of Steve, the Security Guard.

"Yes," I nod. "That's the man who showed us the gun, zip-tied us, then took all our stuff and put it in the other office."

I tell him how we escaped and what our plan was. I don't really know the woman Eric saw in the Foundation Office. I don't know who put the note into my backpack or when. Any time I try to ask the officer a question, he just talks about an ongoing investigation. I'm free to go, but wish I could learn more.

I start out with a hunch, "You know Steve and his accomplice probably cleaned out the Foundation fund, thousands of dollars, maybe hundreds of thousands. The office was so messy because they were looking for some kind of cheat sheet with the computer codes. I bet that they needed time to break the code before transferring the money to a safe place. That's what the hoax was about, a diversion for embezzlement. Once done, they just needed to flee the country. They can pick up their money any place." The officer doesn't say anything, but nods.

Emboldened by the nod, I continue, "But Steve can't leave, because he knew that Eric walked in on his accomplice. He had to discredit Eric, so he slipped the fire crackers in Eric's backpack. Steve and whoever had to stick around long enough to delete all the proof on the security tapes before hitting the road. He had until Friday to hand over the digital video logs to the police. I think we just messed with his time line."

The officer has been nodding the entire time. "Have you thought about going into police work?" He smiles. "You have the mind of a good detective. I think you are on the right track and since all of you have been cleared, I can tell you that we have an APB out for Steve. His records show he has an older sister who has been out of work for a few years. She happens to be a wiz in the technology field." The officer pauses until the interpreter is finished so we can lock eyes.

OMG! He's saying I'm on the right track.

The police officer continues, "She lost her job when the most recent tech bubble burst. We suspect they're traveling together. We know their car's make and model. Plus, they can't get on a plane without ID. I don't think they planned on having this kind of setback. They're even on a no-fly list. So, we're on it."

As I'm let out of the inner office, I can see that the custodians have put everything back and it looks like nothing was disrupted (other than the tape and the big hole in the glass). And there is Nathan, standing outside the Foundation Office, leaning up against a column reading from his phone. He looks up and smiles. He signs "need" and "help" but doesn't move his eyebrows so it either means "Do you need some help?" or "You need some help." While I'm sure he means the first one, I'm betting he is right about the latter.

I was the last in so the last out. Except I look around and don't see Eric. I don't even have time to get nervous before he strolls from the office, a huge grin on his face. "No more a person of interest. They know I'm innocent." Eric announces, finishing his comment with a Deaf applause. We all applaud as well, interpreters included. Eric freezes his 'applause' in mid-air when he spots Nathan. He then looks at me.

Hmmmm, looks like there needs to be an introduction.

"Eric, this is Nathan," I sign.

I then turn to Nathan and sign, "This is E-R-I-C." I spell out Eric's name slowly so Nathan can get it. Nathan uses his fourth week of ASL signing skills. "Nice to-meet you," he signs.

"Nice to-meet you" Eric copies back just as slowly as Nathan. I give Eric a don't-be-a-jerk glare and he just looks at me as innocently as a newborn.

While I'm shaking my head at Eric, my phone vibrates in my hand.

Nathan is typing… "Are you going to reading class?"

"Reading?" I'm shocked. I take a second look at my phone; 1:00 PM. "What? It's just 1:00 PM? I thought it would be dark out."

"That's what I like about you. You pack a lot into one day. I'm curious to see what you'll do tomorrow." He gives me that smile. "Come on, I'll walk you to class and get you something to eat on the way."

"Walk me to class, yes, but I'll get you lunch for coming all this way just to walk me." I smile back at him.

"Deal," he says.

While Nathan and I are typing back and forth, grinning at each other, I notice Eric looking at me very carefully. No grin on his face. I sign to him that I'm going to reading class. I ask him if he is. Oh, the look I get back. The expression says, are you kidding me? After this morning, he wants a nap. Maybe two. He is going straight home.

Quick hugs all around and Nathan and I are on our way. The police will take care of Steve and his sister.

Chapter 14

The next day, a long run is refreshing to my body and spirit. Things are finally getting back on track. I get loads of studying done after my run. I play a few games of tennis, badly, with Rachel just for the fun of being together outside. Friday morning I see Nathan in biology and almost blush. Blush! Sure, I have not dated a lot of guys, but I'm acting as if this is the first date I have ever been on. I have to play it cool. Or at least keep the blush under control.

After my last class on Friday, I receive a text to go to the Security Office at 4:00 P.M. Of course, I'm curious to learn if there is any news between the Security Office and the police about the strange events of the week. Crazy, has it been only one week? No matter what I learn, I will have to get out of here in time for my date with Nathan. After walking with him to my reading class, I don't see Nathan again until this morning in biology. We text nightly, but only about our families or what is happening at school.

I get a text from the Head of Security to meet after my last class at 3:00. I wonder what for and if there will be an interpreter. I doubt Dr. Soto knows how to sign. I head over after class.

"Hello dear, long time no kidnapped…haha" Franz greets me.

"Yeah, I've been able to sleep these last few nights," I laugh.

"Alone," Franz teases me. "Or with Mr. Wonderful who whisked you away on Wednesday?"

"How did you know," I mug, looking shocked. "Right after reading we jetted off to the Bahamas for a fling. I tried to hide it from you, but you know me too well."

We're laughing when Rachel and Eric arrive. None of us know what this is about. We each received the same text. We knock on the door and the interpreter Janet is already there. Dr. Soto is there along with a young man who lights up when he sees Rachel, then me, then Rachel again. Oh, yeah, this guy is confused.

I raise my eyebrows to my sister and fingerspell, "Dave?"

She gives me that sisterly, 'don't you dare' look and I know I'm right. Dave is about six feet tall with very cropped dark brown hair and beautiful brown skin. He's not fat, but solid and muscular. He has these big, deep brown eyes with the longest lashes I've seen outside a Maybelline commercial. No wonder my sister noticed him.

Two people stand up when we enter, one holding a no nonsense camera.

Dr. Soto speaks and gestures grandly as if addressing a larger audience than just the few of us. "I wonder if you can do a favor for us? This is Troy and Becky from the 'Tandy Times' who are interested in having your pictures taken, with me," she adds humbly, as if accepting an academy award. "They want to feature us and also have us answer a few questions. Does that work for everyone? Splendid."

The absence of a pause between the request and the 'splendid' shows that it is not really a request. We're simply expected to smile for the camera. We line up on either side of the Head of Security. The interpreter stands by the camera person, Becky, and translates things like "You…over there," "closer," and "say cheese."

I'm eager to learn what the reporter, Troy, knows about the ongoing investigation, so I'm willing to play along with his questions until I can slip in a couple of my own. He leads us through the events starting with Eric being blamed for the hoax that causes a campus lockdown, through my note, the kidnapping, and the police intervention Wednesday afternoon.

"With campus security assisting," Dr. Soto interjects.

My turn. "Have you been able to learn from the police what has happened to the security officer, Steve? Was he apprehended?" I ask.

"No, but the police think he is long gone. They caught the sister," the reporter explains. "She was the brains of the duo. Well, maybe not the brains since she drove her own car to the Portland airport. While waiting for a flight at PDX, she was picked up…laptop and all."

"They have her?" I ask, shocked. I look at Dr. Soto who just stares right back at me.

"We're not at liberty to share information about an ongoing investigation," she says.

I turn my back to her and focus on Troy, who obviously has a way of getting the police to talk. "Did she confess?" I ask him.

"She didn't really have to. They had her laptop and probable cause. As soon as the police got a warrant, they found out all they needed on where the money was. She transferred," he flips through his notebook again, "half a million dollars from the Foundation fund. Cleaned it out. If not for all of you, hundreds of students would be without the needed scholarships for next year alone. With all the information there, the police were able to get back every cent. Chenoa owes you four a big debt of gratitude."

"And Steve Wallace?" I ask.

"Stacie Wallace told police that since they would be looking for two people, she would drive to Portland and he would drive to Eugene. They would fly to Las Vegas and wait there before flying out to a coastal city south of the border, Puerto Nuevo," Troy reads.

"I guess she never learned the 'anything you say can be used against you' part of the Miranda Warning," Rachel chimes in.

"Oh, she lawyered up real fast," the reporter says. "This was not the first time she has been in trouble for doing this kind of thing. All this information was given with her lawyer right there. The police had her. But they didn't have her on kidnapping, which holds a much harsher penalty. She struck a deal. She gets a lighter penalty for telling us everything she can about her brother's plan. The police said that she was genuinely disgusted when she learned Steve had kidnapped you four."

The Head of Security says confidently, "The police know his car, the airport, where he's going and his final destination. We'll get him."

I think her use of 'we' a little heavy handed, but let it go. I just wish they had Steve in custody, too.

"Thanks for coming, you four, and thank you – Janet – for interpreting for us," says Dr. Soto.

It is nice of Soto to thank Janet, but I think it must be weird to have to thank yourself with your own signs, because of course Janet has to interpret the 'thank you' comment.

We exit the Security Office…all except Rachel who lingers a little. I smile as I watch Dave cross the room and start up a conversation with her. We learned all that in about 30 minutes, so I have plenty of time to get home and get ready for tonight.

I step outside and let Dave work his magic on my sister. She's a good judge of character. I sit on a bench nearby so she can see me when she comes out. Since school started, I'm never without something to read. I reach in my backpack, feel for a textbook, and dive in.

Lost in one of the Reading 115 articles, I don't even notice Rachel until she's almost in front of me. She has a big goofy grin on her face. "We're having lunch on Saturday" she signs. "I'm taking it slow. Lunch means you are just getting to know them and are not too serious."

"My sister, the mystery," I smile and realize now our smiles match. We head to the car and then home.

I get dressed while Rachel tells Mom and Dad about the newspaper reporter and camera person and everything we learned about the Wallace siblings. I'm sure Dad is also texting Aunt Wendy, who is always kept in the loop when it comes to her nieces.

Nathan arrives at six. I've been through four outfits to find one that looks casual. He looks handsome and relaxed. Although we spent time between library book stacks while a possible gunman stalked the campus, I'm more nervous now. I introduce him to Mom and Dad; he has already met my sister. I tell my parents that Nathan is in my biology class and that is the extent of what I share. We're not talking about homework tonight. My dad seamlessly takes over interpreting duties as we converse a little about school and different classes. The chuckles help get rid of some of the butterflies which had taken up residency in my stomach.

They say goodbye and we're out the door and off to some pizza place. Not that it is a test, mind you, but there are only two real choices in town according to my family: Tie Dye Pizza and Stella's. I'm wondering which he picks.

Chapter 15

We arrive at Stella's and as soon as we're out of the car, I can smell this crazy combination of fall air and pizza. I breathe in and sign, "I really like it here. My favorite" I sign brushing my fingers across my nose. Nathan does not know what it means so I spell out "f-a-v-o-r-i-t-e."

He copies the sign "favorite" then signs, "me 2" using the sign for number two. I show him the way to sign the concept 'me too' using the "Y" handshape which he copies. Darn, this was not supposed to be a tutoring session. That's okay, I like that he's trying. I hope he doesn't want to hang out just so I can show him signs. I don't like that. I've had people in the past who pretended to be my friend, but all they wanted was cheap tutoring. I shake off the negative memories and refocus on the great smells.

Once we sit down, we take out our phones and I relax. This is the way I'm used to communicating with Nathan.

"Your favorite spot, right?" He types. He sees me nod so continues, "What is your favorite pizza?"

"A-l-l," I fingerspell really big.

"Even the clams???" he texts.

I nod. Then to let him off the hook, I suggest, "What about we share a Pizza Toscana and each get a Caesar salad. They're really good here."

He nods and puts down the menu. The waitperson comes over and Nathan orders for the both of us. When it comes to drinks, I just tap my water glass and make the 'okay' gesture.

She leaves and we get back to typing. "Should we play spin the bottle or 20 questions?" he pushes send, then waits for me to read. I can feel that blush creeping up my neck.

"Well, without a bottle in sight, let's go for six questions, then it will be my turn," I tease and I rub my hands together in a villainous manner.

He begins the questions:

"1. Middle name?"

"Ann."

"2. Favorite Snack?"

"Costco Chicago popcorn – includes both cheese and caramel corn."

He gives this shudder and says, "I'm not big on the new sweet/salty combo."

"Me neither," I clarify. "I eat all the cheese popcorn and then the caramel for dessert," I type with a big grin.

"3. First kiss?"

"Kyle."

"4. When?"

"Second grade."

He looks up from the phone and gives me that one eyebrow up gaze.

"5. Favorite movie?"

"The Secret Life of Walter Mitty."

"6. Favorite music?" He clicks send then looks at me horrified. "I'm so sorry. I didn't mean that. I just forgot. I'm such a jerk."

I lean over and touch his arm then go back to texting. "Don't worry about it. That's kind of nice that you forgot. My favorite song…let me think. 'We will, we will rock you!' I don't know the name, but I love the vibrations and how everybody seems to know it. You know, deafness is not like a light switch: you can hear or you can't. There are plenty of people who are Deaf and can enjoy music. Some can hear sounds but not the words. I really can't hear any of the sounds or words, but I can still feel the vibrations. There were all kinds of dances at the State School for the Deaf. You know the big speakers at old concerts? They put them face down on the wood floor and we would feel it through our whole bodies. Never be afraid to ask questions, okay?" I push send, and see Nathan read through, nodding.

He looks relaxed again. He types, "Okay, your turn."

I started out the same way.

"1. Middle name?"

"Howard," he typed then made a silly face.

"2. Favorite Snack"

"Peanut M&M's, naturally."

"3. Last kiss?" I type and hover over the send button, then click 'send.' He reads what I write and gives me such a startled look, then a chuckle.

"So, you want to go there?" He types.

I nod and he tells me about a friend of the family that he went to the prom with last year. He explains that his father has very wealthy and powerful friends.

"I'm considered a bit of a catch," he bats his eyes at me and I laugh. "I was kind of set up for the good of the family. But she was really nice, smart, pretty. We kissed goodnight and she's off to a fancy college on the East Coast. Is that enough information for you?"

"4. Favorite Movie?"

"Frozen," he says, straight faced. Then he breaks into a smile and types, "The Bourne Trilogy."

I nod. I like those as well. Powerful, action packed.

"5. Favorite music?"

He has to think about that for a while. The salad comes and we start eating. I gesture for him to type between bites, but he holds up a finger and is just deep in thought. Finally he picks up his phone again.

"I can't do this. I like it all. Well, almost all of it. I don't like some country and I don't like some rap. I don't know how to explain it. Either things sound right or move me or…not." I can see he is getting uncomfortable talking about music again.

"I get it. I'm not a fashion queen, but when I put something on I know if I like it or don't like it right away," I explain.

His face brightens. He can tell I understand.

"Last question," I say. He puts his hands in a praying position and looks up to the ceiling.

"6. Ocean or Mountains?"

"Easy one. Ocean," he replies.

I read the message just as the pizza arrives. We spend the next few minutes eating the wonderful pizza and making dreamy faces, not at each other, but at the pizza. It is delicious. While I offer to split the bill, he says that I can pick up the next meal. This makes me feel light as air, as I look across the table at him. The next date.

I sign, "I'm thinking Burger King (but I spelled BK) or McDonald's (using the 'M' handshape to trace two small arches." He gets it right away and laughs.

He fingerspells back, "O.K."

That right there is my favorite part of the date. When we're not typing to each other, just communicating through sign. I know he is taking a class because of his little brother, but I don't know how serious he is about it. That could cause problems down the line. I kick myself mentally. It's just a first date. Let's not be picking out wedding invitations.

Nathan drops me off at the house, leans in for a little kiss. Sweet, no pressure. I head to the house and he waits until I open the door before taking off.

No studying tonight. I'll simply bask in a lovely evening.

Rachel is still up chatting on the phone. She points to the phone and spells, "Dave."

I smile and give her a thumbs-up, get ready for bed, turn off the lights and fall asleep thinking of that kiss. Yup, we didn't have any problems in that area. But communication? Where does that lead us?

Chapter 16

Saturday seems full of chores and homework. Rachel leaves for her lunch date and comes back floating. It seems that she and Dave have a lot in common with what they like to do. I want the whole scoop.

"He loves books as much as I do, if that is even possible. When he was young, his mom and dad got divorced and for a while, Dave escaped into books where he found that people fell in love forever. Mighty men slew dragons and Elven women ran countries."

"Oh, no," I put my wrist up to my forehead in a dramatic pose. "Not another Lord of the Rings enthusiast?"

"Do you want to know about Dave or not?" she asks. I nod slowly, like a child who is asking forgiveness, and she continues. "Dave's dad still lives near and teaches English at Wesley. His mom writes books. She's published! He has two younger sisters. I guess the divorce and having two younger sisters kind of brought the caretaker out in him. He goes to his dad's private school part time while working at Chenoa as a security guard, something that he really enjoys. He has it all planned out. Although he's working part time, he can be done with college at 25 practically debt free. How many students can you say that about?"

"Not many," I agree.

"When it comes to his features and skin tone, he takes after his Hispanic father more than his white mother. His parents don't speak much Spanish, but Dave decided to learn it in high school because so many people just assumed he spoke Spanish. It drove him crazy that people would just come up to him and start speaking Spanish. He also knew that the Hispanic population was growing very fast in Tandy and the areas nearby, so he wanted a second language to bump up the odds of getting a job. Three years of high school Spanish gave him a pretty good foundation. He is continuing Spanish in college. He loves languages and is thinking of being some kind of linguist."

She continued, eyes glowing, "When he and his sisters visit his dad's parents, they get a healthy dose of Spanish. His sisters are not as eager to learn Spanish, so he spends a lot of time being the… interpreter," she smiles.

"I do believe you have a major crush on this guy!" I exclaim in mock horror. "You? Rachel Carn, who does not have time for boys because she must be an author on the New York Times Best Seller List, has a crush?"

"It was just one lunch." Rachel starts to blush.

"So tell me more…where did you go?" I ask.

"Toshi's. You know how long I've wanted to date someone who likes sushi? I mean likes it, not just pretends to like it because I do. He knows about some of the traditions of eating in Japan and we talked about travel and what we wanted out of our education. It was great." She stops for a minute. "Oh, I forgot to tell you. The police are keeping the Chenoa Security in the loop so Dave can tell me what's going on. They never found Steve, but they think he bypassed the Eugene airport and drove straight to Las Vegas. Stacie gave him up, and made a deal with the DA. Since she admitted her part of the scam, she will stay in jail until she is sentenced even though all the money was returned. They still have hope for catching Steve, but they won't be sentenced together. That's all he was able to tell me. That's all Dave knows, but it's better than nothing. I don't think we would get anything from the police because it is 'an ongoing investigation.' Our favorite phrase."

"What about you? Where did you two go last night?" Rachel asks.

"Stella's for pizza," I reply. "We talked a lot, but through our phones. I'm not complaining. He's taking a sign language class this term. I just wish he could sign comfortably. But he's pretty motivated to learn."

"Nice," Rachel nods.

"No, it's not because of me. He, his mom and sister are all taking sign language because Nathan's little brother is autistic. He's recently diagnosed and the doctor thinks it might be a good way to stimulate communication," I explain.

"What does Eric think about all this?" Rachel asks.

"What do you mean?" I sign.

"You know perfectly well what I mean. His crush is written all over his face, and it's been that way since he discovered girls," Rachel says. "Don't act like you are not aware of it."

"Oh, you know I love Eric. He and Franz are my best friends, present company excepted," I do a little bow. "But he feels like my brother. Anyway, he just thinks he's in love with me."

"Ah HA!" my sister fires back. "So you know he's in love with you."

"Okay, okay…but what if we were to…I don't know…date. Firstly, it might be creepy and secondly," I sign, counting on my fingers, "If something goes wrong, I've lost one of my best friends. Also, he knows all my tricks. I could never charm him." I finish my short list looking as if I've already won the argument.

"Sis, all you have to do is take his hand and it would charm the pants off him." She smiles. "The pants right off him."

"I don't know," I groan. "Nathan is perfect in every way. He's very classy, funny, and when I was in danger, or rather when he thought I was in danger, he came to be with me. How many people can say that? And he likes me. Me."

"Why wouldn't he?" Rachel said, "You're smart, beautiful....just look at that face."

We dissolve into giggles and that's it for the serious dish. Yet, I can't help but think about what she said. It's always been in the back of my mind; she just brought it forward. I saw a movie where two best friends made a pact that if they were not married by the time they turned 30, they would marry each other.

Was I keeping Eric in the friend zone as a back-up? That's not really fair. I love Eric too much to be treating him like this. But what if Nathan learns sign as well as Rachel? I know of some Deaf/hearing marriages that have worked out.

Oh my gosh, I'm doing it again. I'm 18. I want to be a veterinarian which means I need to focus on my studies. Nathan did ask me for a second date, but maybe he's just interested in my signing. I mean he's taking an ASL class and suddenly he has me and a small group of signers around him. I'm not saying he wants a free tutor. We had a good date. But how close can we be if we have to type everything? I can hardly get to sleep because of all the options in my head. Tomorrow will be a better day. I will put both guys out of my head and focus on reading, math, and biology.

*

Sunday is the perfect autumn day, with the trees the most glorious colors. Tandy has the perfect ratio of trees that change colors versus the trees and bushes that stay the same all year round. Azaleas and Rhododendrons bloom once a year, but the rest of the time the green stays that way. There are cedars and fir in abundance, which makes a perfect backdrop for the red, orange, and yellow, no, golden leaves. We have this wonderful plant in the back yard that you see all over town which grows as high as many trees. It's green throughout year round, even under the snow (if we get any). But its new growth is red, a biologist's dream. In addition to that, once a year it grows tiny white blossoms.

I get on my gear and do some running to clear my head. Just three or so miles.

Digging into studies after a run always feels as if I'm studying with a full charge. I spend about an hour on each class and am feeling ready for the week. I wonder if Aunt Wendy would like some company. I text and we set up a time. She'll come pick me up.

Rachel has the car at the library and won't be back for a while. Her tennis team gets together for what they call 'team building' each Sunday afternoon. It's just an excuse to drink coffee or soda and eat whatever snacks are still at the Governor's Cup. There might be something about the whole team building thing, because they sure do have a good time.

Aunt Wendy picks me up and we head back to her home for tea. Once we're there and have set out the tea and cookies, I begin. My Aunt is one of the coolest adults I know. She doesn't rush into anything and allows me to sort it out as I'm sharing. She just listens and waits. Finally I get around to Nathan and the great date we had and how he asked me to go on another one. No specific time, just hinted at a future date. She nods and I'm encouraged to go on.

"Well, I was talking with Rachel and she asked me about Eric." I look down at my nails then back up to her. "You know I love Eric. I just don't think I love him the way he wants me to love him. I guess I'm asking for more than someone to listen. I need to know what to do." I drop my hands in my lap.

"Only you know what you need to do," Aunt Wendy says.

"Be honest with Eric and tell him how I feel?" I ask.

"Are you guessing or knowing?" she says with a smile.

She is right, I know what to do. Eric is too good a friend. I have to be honest – really honest.

"I have to be honest with Eric and also honest with myself. I do like Eric, but I'm not ready to like him the way he wants." I finish, and wait for Aunt Wendy to respond.

"That sounds honest," she says. "Now tell me about these criminals. Most importantly, give me the scoop on your sister and this Dave fellow. Your dad says she's humming around the house. Humming."

I bring her up to date on all that has been going on with Rachel and what she heard from Dave. I don't tell her everything I know about how Rachel feels because that is her information to share.

We continue to share for over an hour. I learn what is going on at the State School for the Deaf, Aunt Wendy's writing, and different events with friends. It is the perfect visit for a break from a big day of studying. But now, back to work for me. She drives me home and we say our goodbyes.

After I get back to studying, I receive two texts, one from Nathan and one from Eric. Oh no, I groan, six months of no dating and then two guys in two weeks. Nathan wants me to come over after school tomorrow and meet his mom, sis, and brother. Hummm, I wonder, why not his father. There is a story there. He says it's about his mom not believing sign language will help and she's giving up. He doesn't want that to happen. That's a little strange. I'm not Ms. Deaf America with magic tricks. But, I can at least be there to support him.

I let Nathan know that I'd be glad to meet his mom. "I'll come from school with my sister but we can't really stay too long." That sounds kind of cold. I delete the text and try again. "We'll be glad to swing by after our last class. See you." Okay that sounds better, supportive and yet letting him know I'm not his tutor just because he's adorable.

Eric wants dinner Wednesday night. Usually he just texts me when he invites the whole gang for pizza. This is clearly for me specifically. He is going to pick me up. Pick me up? We have known each other since the second grade. I have homework!

I text Eric that Wednesday night at 6:00 P.M. will be just fine.

I put my phone to the side and dare it to vibrate until I get two full hours done. It vibrates, but I let it go until just before bedtime. I WILL be a veterinarian.

Chapter 17

Monday almost flies by with my eyes towards midterms. I ask Rachel if we can go for a quick drive by to see Nathan after school and beg her to interpret for the whole gang of us. She's usually right there beside me anytime someone can't sign, but I know that interpreting and signing are two different things. We can sign the night away, but interpreting the words of other people, having their thoughts and emotions go through one's body, that's a whole different thing.

"I'll load and unload the dishwasher for a week," I beg. She laughs and agrees.

We meet at the car after class and Rachel has this weird expression on her face.

"Are you gloating because I have to do your chores for a week?" I pout.

"It's a little more complicated than that, but we have to talk before we see Nathan," Rachel says, then wipes a grin off her face.

"What have you done, Sis?" I'm starting to get a little peeved.

"Okay, Okay," she starts. "I'm going through Building 3 for my drawing class, and before I know what is happening, someone slips an arm around my waist. I'm suddenly nose to nose with Nathan who leans in and…"

"What?" I ask, when she stops mid-sentence.

"Well," she grits her teeth. "He kinda kisses me."

"Kisses you?" I sign, my jaw dropping.

"Of course! He thought it was YOU. I said, 'What the heck,' or…or something and as soon as he heard my voice he was mortified. I mean MORTIFIED. He blushed and stammered, apologized about seven or eight different times. Come on, we'll be able to laugh about this in 60 years or so."

"He saw me this morning," I said. We're not dressed anything alike." I sign, still flustered.

"Really, guys notice clothes? What was Nathan wearing this morning in biology?"

I realized I could not remember. "Good point," is all I say.

"Fair kisser," Rachel said, then with big eyes adds, "Too soon?"

I shake my head and we both chuckle while getting into the car. We head to South Tandy and then on River Road past the Tandy Golf club. As the houses get more expensive, I start getting butterflies in my stomach. We head east, towards the Talula River and find Nathan's home…er…mansion. Rachel and I look at each other and think we're probably way underdressed. I mean WAY underdressed.

Rachel pulls into the driveway and asks me, "What do Nathan's parents do?"

"He said his father was a lawyer," I explain. "He didn't say about his mom. The whole process with doctors and the autistic diagnosis has been a steep learning curve for the whole family."

"Well," Rachel signs, "He's either a really good lawyer or a really bad one."

"Haha," I reply, giving her a gentle push before we get out of the car and head to the house.

Nathan is there to greet us, and I see a blush rise from his collar.

"My sister told me about the…mix up. We do need big name tags," I smile at him to let him know all is okay among the three of us.

We step into his family's beautiful home. A woman about our mom's age, walks confidently, and might I say, elegantly towards us.

"Why! Aren't you beauties?" She smiles, I understand you are Elizabeth and Rachel Carn. One of you is Deaf and has stolen my Nathan's heart."

"Mom!" Nathan turns full-on blush.

"You have a lovely home, Mrs. Graham," I sign and Rachel voices what I say.

The mother is a little taken aback seeing one person sign and hearing the other person speak. But, she recovers quickly and leads us into the living room. "Please call me Maxine."

A rather pretty girl sits quietly in the living room. She looks about 10 years old. No fidgeting, she appears shy, but has her own kind of elegance about her. Once Nathan sits down, she goes over and sits next to him.

"This is my daughter, Emily," Maxine points out. "Benjamin may or may not join us, depending on his mood and how safe he feels with new people in the house. First, I want to take this opportunity to thank both of you for coming over right from Chenoa. Nathan tells me you both have busy schedules."

"We're glad to be here and may I say, my sister is being wonderful to come along with me as our interpreter. While we know a great deal about ASL, American Sign Language, we know very little about autism. We don't exactly know how we can help, but appreciate your wanting to see us." Frankly, I didn't know what else to say.

Always a perfect host, apparently, Maxine, asks us if we would like anything to eat or drink. She asks her daughter to bring out water for everyone. Emily comes in with these small water bottles on a tray and hands them out. Her mom's eyes follow her, proud of the small host she is raising.

Maxine starts the next part as if she has practiced it. "Benjamin was diagnosed on the autistic spectrum about six months ago. Since he was about two years old, we noticed some things he did and learned were very different from Nathan and Emily. Now, we know all kids are different and accept that to be the case, but after a couple of years we started noticing more and more things that were different. He is healthy, smart, and curious, which is wonderful. However his language development has been painfully slow which frustrates all of us. I'm very scared that the more he can't communicate, the further he will drift from wanting to communicate. The doctors suggested that we learn sign language to help stimulate his communication. Now the Huffington Post just came out with an article that summarizes about 20 studies and reports, rather convincingly, that tend to prove using images can help the child communicate better than sign language. We have been taking ASL classes five weeks now and we still know very little, and nothing has sparked Bennie's imagination. We don't know if we should stop the ASL classes or not."

"Just to be clear," Nathan pipes in, "I never said I was going to stop taking ASL. Whatever Mom decides for herself, I'm still taking it."

I give Nathan a smile and turn my attention back to his mother. "Do you voice when you use the signs with each other and with Benjamin?" I ask.

"Of course," the mother says.

"Was there anything in the article about more than one system being confusing or detrimental to the child?"

"Noooo…not that I recall," she replies.

"Is there something in the process that would keep you from using everything you can to stimulate his communication: pictures, voice, and signs?" I ask.

Nathan's mom just sits there deep in thought. She then, in a rather uncharacteristic manner, whoops and claps her hands together. "Yes, do all three. Why not? This is why I need to get back in the office again. The give-and-take of all those people brainstorming fresh ideas is what I need. I feel my ideas are growing old."

"One more thing I want to interject before we leave," I explain. "There is a difference between American Sign Language (ASL), gestures, and what some call Signed English. ASL has its own grammatical structure, different from English. You will learn more and more about that if you continue to take the class. But since your goal is to help Benjamin move his communication from sounds and gestures to speech, you may wish to use the signs you are learning in ASL, but use them as best you can in English order. When my sister signs and talks at the same time, she is changing her ASL into more signed English. However, when we're talking with each other, we use ASL. I don't mean this to keep you from taking the ASL class. You'll learn great signs there, but I just want you to know that you will be learning a different grammatical structure….one that is very difficult, if not impossible to use when you add your voice. I didn't scare you, did I?"

"Not at all," Maxine smiles, "Just more information for me to think about. More information is never a bad thing. Thank you. I know you want to get along home but would you like a short tour? I'm sure Nathan and Emily would be happy to show you around."

I look over to Rachel who nods her head enthusiastically. My sister loves the arts, writing, poetry and the like. The paintings on the walls alone could fund both years of CCC for each of us, and we have only seen the entry way and the living room.

Nathan and Emily take us around the house and out to the heated pool and hot tub while we sip on our waters. Rachel looks over a string of books in the den.

"Careful," I tell Nathan. "She loves books even more than I do."

"Good thing," he said, laughing, or my mom would lose her business."

Rachel asks me if she can interject something, I nod. The whole process just takes a second. "Nathan, I'm talking for me, Rachel."

"Shoot," he replies.

"Does your mother have a bookstore in Tandy? I thought I knew every bookstore." Rachel asks as we walk back to the living room. We notice Benjamin, about five years old, peeking around corners here and there.

"No, she started a small publishing company when I was young and she wanted to have more time for yours truly," he says.

"What's the name of the company?" Rachel asks.

"Max Howard Publishing," he answers.

Rachel freezes in mid-step. "Are you kidding me? Maxine, your mom, is THE Max of Max Howard?"

Chapter 18

"His middle name is Howard," I tell Rachel. Nathan looks at me and raises that one eye brow. "Oh, was that a secret?" I grimace. "Sorry. It really is a nice middle name."

"Exactly," Nathan's mom makes another elegant entrance. "When you are playing with the big boys, you have to have a strong name. I would have never printed my first book had I named my publishing company, 'Missy Maxine.' I would have been laughed out of the business."

Rachel is still signing and talking, but I can hardly make out her signs. I thought she was going to curtsey.

"I love your books!" Rachel gushes. "You know, Nathan, your mom says the word and any book she touches goes straight to Hollywood. She is the number one expert on Young Adult fiction on the entire west coast. She's won an award for the top grossing YA fiction the last four years in a row."

"I like these young ladies very much," Maxine smiles. "My dear, you have a better memory for my resume than I do. Honestly, I have been very lucky to work with such great writers and have had my share of wonderful mentors. For coming all this way to educate me and put my mind to rest, would you like me to autograph a copy of one of your favorites?" Maxine graciously offers.

"I wouldn't know which one to pick." Rachel looked at the long row of books. "I love them all. No, here it is: *The Sailor and the Piano Teacher*, Bowman and Hawk, second edition." Rachel picks it out and hands it over to Maxine.

"Little known fact," Maxine said, "Do you know about the cover?"

Rachel, speechless, shakes her head no.

"Well, since you have read it, you know it's a collection of letters. I found the book through a friend of mine, Hawk, who is a historian buff. There was much going on during those months the letters covered from World War II, both in battles and overseas. I contacted Bowman and we collaborated on a second edition bringing in Hawk who was able to add historical information. But the cover, we kept the same as the original. Bowman takes pictures of her home-grown roses on her sister's piano with a cell phone. Voila, the cover. It could not be more symbolically perfect, the same color and kind of roses her father gave her mother on their first date." Maxine finishes signing the book and hands it over to Rachel.

After many 'thank you's,' Rachel gets her book and floats out to the car.

"I'm driving now," I say firmly. "I don't see how your feet can touch the pedals."

"Can you believe it," Rachel says, "I met Max Howard and Max is FEMALE! What a great woman. Maybe I'll be able to intern in her place in a few years. That's just the kind of work I want to do."

I'm used to this kind of passion from my sister, the writer/poet/artist. She sees such possibilities. Every few months she uses the phrase "That's the kind of work I want to do." Rachel hugs the book and doesn't say a word the rest of the way home.

*

Wednesday in biology class, we're slammed with two extra chapters more than what we're used to covering per week. The pressure is mounting. It's now a usual thing for Nathan and me to be sitting together. At the end of class he pulls out his phone as I do mine, a little tradition we started. Wow, we already have a tradition. He asks if I want to get together for some study time tonight. Awkward.

"How about Thursday," I ask. "Eric and I are having pizza tonight," I type. I mean, I have to be honest with both of them. Really, I don't know how to do this any other way.

He reads the text twice, or very slowly, then types, "Do I have anything to worry about?"

"Eric and I have been close friends since the second grade." I tell him, hoping I'm vague enough.

"Thursday night is ASL. What about Friday? We could grab a bite to eat at the Food Station and then head up to the library for a study session where we test each other on the new chapters. We will have read them by then," Nathan suggests.

I ease up a little. That sounds wonderful. "Sure. That would be super. Remember, I'm buying." I click send and give him a smile.

"Oh no," he shakes his head. "This is not a date. This is a work session. WORK. No funny business."

Straight faced, I raise my left hand and cross my heart with the index finger of my right hand.

Nathan smiles and gets up to go with a 'see you later' sign. We go our separate ways.

I meet the 'gang' for lunch. We talk sports, current events, recent movies, etc. NO talk of homework during these breaks.

Later I have math and reading. Math is going so well, I'm glad I took advanced classes all the way through my senior year in high school. The reading class is not as much work as I thought it would be. The focus is on argument and logic. These are great tools for scientists to have. We also learn study strategies that help me get the most out of textbooks, whatever the topic.

Rachel and I head home after her last class. I'm already getting nervous about my date with Eric. I mean, I think he made it clear that it was a date. What if he tries to kiss me? Kissing Eric. I'm sure

I've thought of it before. There were times growing up when I had a crush on him and he wasn't interested or vice versa. But that was when we were kids. It's different now. Do I dress like it's a date? If it was the gang, I'd throw on my jeans and a T-shirt and run a brush through my hair. Do I wear a dress? I don't even wear a dress for school. This is already way too complicated.

I work through my closet…like some kind of fashion Goldilocks….this is tooooooo formal, this is toooooo casual. Ah, this is just right. I finally go for casual clothes, but my hair and makeup are a little more formal. I go through all this and picture Eric smelling a T-shirt he picked up off the floor, nodding, then putting it on. I'm such a goof.

The doorbell rings/flashes and I'm on my way. Rachel has been upstairs the entire time talking with Mom and Dad. Probably about Nathan's mother. Frankly, my sister would be the better match for his family. Where did that thought come from? I shake my head. It's just nerves and dating two guys at the same time.

I wave bye to the family and open the door. I'm wrong; Eric looks great. Not too formal, but you can tell he has on a clean shirt, different from his usual T-shirt collection. Thank goodness I did my hair.

"Hi," he smiles. "Your hair looks great."

"Thanks," I reply. Yes, this just got weird.

We head out to the car and he drives to Tie Dye Pizza. I start to relax, because this is not really a formal place and the gang often comes here together. Eric knows how I like my pizza, which is different from him – a straight pepperoni man. We get double slices, a soda, and sit down at one of the booths.

The pizza is divine as usual. Show me a better pesto sauce in this entire town and I will be shocked. We talk of school, how he was framed, and our families. I catch him up on Stacie Wallace, the accomplice they have in jail awaiting for sentencing.

"Hard to believe it was just a few weeks ago," Eric says. "Thanks for being such a powerful advocate and believing in me."

"We all did. Rachel, Franz, my family, your family." I counter. "No one thought…oh yeah, I knew that guy would snap one day."

We both laugh.

"That's when you started seeing Nathan, right?" Eric asks.

Danger, danger, red flags flying up everywhere. "Oh, we knew each other from biology class, but that is the first time I spent so much time with him. We were in that library for a long time.

"How do you communicate?" he asks.

I look down at the table and have to stifle a laugh. Two plates, two glasses, two napkins and two phones. "The same way I talk with you most days," I say, picking up and then wiggling my phone at him.

"Is it serious?" he asks, a wrinkle deepening on his forehead.

"It's been one date." I look at him and ask, "What is your point?"

"Well, this is one date, so I guess we're tied," he says as if he had made his point.

"What?" I'm starting to get mad. "I'm not some kind of prize at the end of the race. We've known each other eleven years and you have never once asked me on a date. Never. Once. Suddenly I go on a date with Nathan and you are asking me about our communication? We have done nothing but talk about Nathan, but on Nathan's date, we didn't talk about you."

I had gone too far, but I was mad. I could see the pain in his eyes.

"I just always thought," he signs, low and privately, "Our friendship would grow into something else. I'm sorry. I guess I'm really jealous because I have had you to myself, in a way. I just thought it would be you and me."

All my anger evaporates in the face of his honesty. He has been my best friend and family for so many years. Maybe I always thought he would be there, too. How would I feel if he started dating someone else?

"But we've never even kissed," I tell him. Yes, I'm being shameless. "Maybe you would be horrible at it. Jessica said you were a bad kisser."

"We were eight years old! I must defend my honor!"

With that he leans over the table and kisses me right on the mouth.

Chapter 19

I know it seems juvenile to say 'right on the mouth' but it was a shock. I had to gather my wits about me.

"Well, that was a surprise," I say. "I think Jessica has a lot of explaining to do."

We sit there grinning at each other. Then I start feeling guilty. Eric could read me, and reaches out to touch my arm. "It's okay. I just thought it was important that I let you know how I feel. I would hate to live a life where I wasn't honest. I don't think I have been honest about you."

"Wow, this is the most serious first date I've ever been on," I quip, trying to lighten the mood. "I really don't know how I feel. And, I don't know when I'll know. You know my goal is to be a vet. That is my number one goal. Everything else takes a back seat to that. I'm trying to be honest, too."

"Eat your second slice before it gets cold," Eric says, and we spend the next few minutes eating lovely pizza and enjoying each other's company.

I must admit it is fun taking a trip down memory lane. I don't know if it is just fun and games or if Eric is trying to make a point that we have a lot of history together. I have to admit having free communication and not having to type the entire date is a relief. We also talk about his psychology class. He is learning a lot of things that are pushing him to be more introspective. That's a pretty good step for carefree Eric.

After pizza, we head home. He knows how dedicated I am to my studies so doesn't try to keep me out "on a school night." He walks me to the door. Really Eric, you are definitely showing me this is a date, not just hanging out. On the doorstep, he leans over and gives me a sweet kiss. I must admit it is even better than the first.

"I just need to break the tie," he signs, a wicked grin on his face. I shake my finger at him, but have a smile on my face as well.

"Drive safely," I sign and unlock the front door. I hug Mom and Dad, who are still up. They ask me if I had fun, and I say, "Yep, good time."

I can't wait to find Rachel. She has a bunch of papers spilled out on the table in front of the TV in our game room. She looks up to sign "Hi" then takes a closer look at my goofy grin. I tell her about the evening.

"He did WHAT?" my sister said.

"I KNOW," I sign back. "Twice!"

"WHAT? Twice? Did you like it?" she asks. Seeing my expression she bounces up and down on the love seat. "You did. You liked it. Two boys in one week. You know what we call those kinds of girls???...Lucky." She starts laughing again.

"They're both great," I groan and plop my head into the throw pillow. "I don't know what to do."

*

Thursday, another long run. I can't believe I get credit for doing something I would do anyway. As online students, we learn about the health benefits of running and then we track our time/miles. It's a great idea for people like me who like the credit and will run or exercise anyway. I wonder if any students take advantage of reporting their own minutes/miles. Friday passes without drama; no one kisses me or my sister, thinking it's me. No dates, except for a study date with Nathan. No funny business. I promise. I smile to myself.

Rachel has a date with Dave for Saturday night. For two artist types, things are going very smoothly. They text nightly and seem to enjoy each other's company. This Saturday they are going to a gallery opening. It appears that a relatively new art gallery, Blue Raven, has moved from Ferry Street to a better location on Liberty. The artists are pulling out all the stops with art demonstrations, free refreshments, and live music. She's looking forward to the evening.

I spend some time on the phone each night with Franz, Nathan, and Eric. Franz lets the funny emoji's fly as I explain what happened with both Nathan and Eric. I also tell her about my sister's 'shero' worship of Nathan's mother, the publisher. I ask Franz if she asked the cute blonde from the library out.

"Nah, she's straight and hearing. Two strikes and I'm out," she laments. Not that many gay and Deaf people in the area that she has not already met or dated. We thought at college she would meet more gay Deaf people, but most of those are guys.

"Someday she'll come along." I tell her, "Don't be discouraged."

"Says the girl dating two guys," Franz teases.

Friday after class, I text Aunt Wendy and ask her if she is willing to host one of her famous dinners. I volunteer to help with any kind of clean up before and after. Monday is midterms, and I have to buckle down. What about the Wednesday after midterms? I ask if we could expand the usual five and invite Nathan and Dave. She thinks it is a splendid idea, but says that we would need some interpreters. "Your sister will want to be a participant and not work. I have two in mind that owe me a big favor. Maybe they can come. I'll get back to you."

Nathan and I meet at the Food Station, get a bite to eat, and head to the library.

"Can't believe it is almost two weeks since the lockdown." I tell him.

"I know! Actually, two competing ideas," he types. "It seems like so long ago, and yet I feel as if I'm learning ASL so slowly. I thought it would be faster than this."

I nod, "Many people do. Hearing people often see deaf people using a signed English because it is easier for us to communicate with hearing people that way. It looks like speaking English and just miming. But it's much more complex than that. Think of it as learning Japanese while ice skating." I hit send.

He laughs when he reads what I type. "I know we're here to study biology, but I have a quick question about ASL. Then we'll get to biology." He texts me and solemnly crosses his heart.

I type back, "Shoot."

"What is the deal with 'big D' and 'little d' in the spelling of Deaf? At first I thought it was just poor editing, but then I don't know." He hits send.

"You noticed that. It's a secret Deaf code." I hit send and try to keep a straight face. He reads the text and gives me this look and I bust out in a grin.

"Ha ha," he mouths.

"There are a lot of deaf people in the world. Some are born deaf; some become deaf after they have acquired their first language, and some slowly become deaf as they age. There are many deaf people who believe in (or at least their parents believed in) something called the oral method. Decades ago it was thought that if a child signed, he or she would not learn to speak. So deaf children were taught to take advantage of any type of hearing they had left, often with amplification. They were taught to speak through drills, tongue placement, breath control. It worked for some but not for everyone. Those who did not learn to speak clearly were labeled 'failures' and allowed to sign. You can imagine generations being called 'failures.' Signing was forbidden and punished in these oral schools. Aunt Wendy's friend remembers when her thumbs were tied every morning for speech class so she would not be tempted to use her hands. Horrible. But, like I said, that was decades ago. Oral schools now use cutting edge technology for hearing devices and cochlear implants and special feedback equipment that makes learning to speak more fun. It's a challenge, no matter how advanced the technology. However, these deaf people identify themselves with the hearing culture and often never sign," I type.

"Sorry, I didn't know it was such a complex issue. I didn't think you would have to text a book," Nathan texts back.

"Okay, Deaf people who believe ASL is a full, real language and the natural language of the Deaf use the 'big D' to identify themselves and their culture, which includes seeing themselves not as broken, but just different. So your grandpa who has lost his hearing is 'deaf' while I'm 'Deaf.'" I text, "Does that answer your question?"

"Yes, and thank you," Nathan texts. "I also have this text to refer back to. Thanks, Elizabeth. Okay, biology."

He is sure honest when he says no funny business. We get down to work and study well together. He brought index cards that we used like a game, old school. We write a vocabulary word to the other and that person has to define it, draw a picture of it, or explain how it is used in a process.

We work two hours moving the cards back and forth between us. This guy matches my passion for learning this stuff. After two hours he walks me to my car, gives me a kiss, and sees that I'm safely 'tucked in.'

When I arrive home, I have a text message from Aunt Wendy. Everyone is a go except she doesn't have Nathan's or Dave's contact information. I tell her we'll ask the guys and then thank her about 100 times on the text.

It is one of those rare times, maybe because midterms are almost over, that everyone can come, even the interpreters. Nathan and Dave have never been to a party where they are the minority and everyone else can sign. I think it's important to see how they handle the situation. I text Nathan who accepts. I'll talk to Rachel when she gets home.

Rachel comes home later and I sign, "Your turn. Tell me all about it."

Rachel has a great time with Dave at the gallery opening, there is no special theme, other than 'welcome.' There is something for everyone. Dave leans towards the more traditional painters and photographers. Rachel, on the other hand, being a big fan of abstracts, is in her element. After the show they stop at the Dolce Bakery for a slice of decadent cake and a cup of tea.

She gets this dreamy look in her eyes when she talks about the two of them being able to talk, just talk, all night.

"And you only talked?" I ask.

"Wellll," she fingerspells 'wellll' using several "l" letters. "After the gallery we walked along Liberty and looked at all the shop windows, discussing how we would make them better. We stopped a few times. I must admit, he's good at stopping just at the right place." She smiles and wiggled her eyebrows up and down. "I'll text him and invite him to Aunt Wendy's party."

During the weekend, other than some texts, I have no dates, no pizza, no surprise kisses. I'm in full-on study mode, and I don't miss a social life at all. Not much.

Midterms come and go (biology on Monday and reading on Wednesday). Rachel has two exams on Monday and one on Tuesday. I leave school with the car and zip over to Aunt Wendy's house. "Just hiding all the knives," she smiles when letting me in, "In case Eric and Nathan decide to have a duel." I give her a childish squint. These gatherings happen enough times that I know where everything is and ask if she wants me to set the table. Aunt Wendy has this amazing table in the middle of her dining room. Rachel and I would play with it until it drove the adults mad. Instead of a table that widened by the use of leaves, the table top would move clockwise and get bigger with different cleverly cut parts popping up. You could move it counter-clockwise to make it shrink.

As a Deaf person who uses American Sign Language, I find it helpful to have a table where everyone can see everyone else. You don't have to be near to hear someone, but you need to be able to see them. Aunt Wendy tells me to set up for nine, which requires dragging in chairs from other rooms. Once the table is set, I do this and that as she requests. Our Aunt Wendy is the only one I know who serves dinner with paper plates and crystal glasses on fine linens. She does not give a hoot about what others think of her and she hates washing plates, but likes washing crystal. That's my Aunt. The two hours fly by. When people start arriving, I slip into the bathroom for a quick face wash, hair comb, and lipstick.

I greet the two interpreters, Sara, from CCC I already knew. The other young woman, Barbara, is from Portland. Once everyone arrives, Aunt Wendy takes charge of the group and seats everyone.

Chapter 20

Aunt Wendy sets the stage by explaining to those who can't sign about the interpreting process and that there is something called 'lag time.'

"As wonderful as these interpreters are, they cannot read anyone's mind, so they have to see what the Deaf people sign before changing it to English. Be patient with the lag. The same thing is true with speaking English and it being translated into ASL," Aunt Wendy explains and then signs, "Let the fun begin. Come nieces, help me bring out the food."

The three of us disappear into the kitchen and come out with lasagna, yummy garlic bread (Aunt Wendy doesn't give a hoot about bad breath at a party), and a large salad. Everyone digs in family style with thank you's to the chef.

"I got the recipe from my Aunt Costco, who makes the best food," she says with an obvious wink. "How is school for all of you? I know most of you go to Chenoa Community College."

Each share what is going on and which classes are liked, which teachers are fun or strict or both.

"Dave," Aunt Wendy asks, "I understand you work part time at CCC and then go to a private college as well. Where do you go?"

"I attend Wesley University south of town. My dad teaches literature classes there so you can't beat the price. My favorite part is that in the literature department they have guest speakers who come in and teach on a rotating basis. We get professors who do seminars for the undergrads, not just the post grads. The homework is at times brutal, but it is so worth it," Dave explains.

I think of the brutal homework and of the midterm I just finished in biology. Both Nathan and I work on making sure each word was drilled into our heads. That is always the hardest thing when you start a new discipline, learning all the technical jargon.

Aunt Wendy knows how to make us all feel comfortable. Nathan tries some of the sign language he is learning, and Dave seems comfortable without knowing any. I knew hearing people in the past who were uncomfortable being in the minority. Dave just seems to take it all in and enjoy himself.

Eric and Nathan pretty much pretend the other does not exist. Nathan is having enough trouble following the conversation, but Eric does not make fun of his signing. As the meal progresses, some questions turn to deafness. Someone asks if deafness is hereditary in my family since both Aunt Wendy and I are Deaf. The answer is that it is not hereditary. We each have different causes of deafness. There are families that have hereditary deafness in them, but ours is not one of them.

Wendy clarifies. "When I was eleven I became very ill with meningitis. Understand, I had already acquired English the way most hearing people do, soaking it up like a little sponge. By eight, one is rather linguistically mature, having trouble with only a couple of structures, like passive structures. I was a hearing girl just living in the early 70's like everyone else. I became sick with meningitis and literally went to sleep hearing and awoke deaf. I was terrified because it was not the norm for me. I also thought it would just go away, like a fever. Of course my parents went all over, doctor after doctor to try and reverse the situation. But I never heard again. Barbara Streisand, "The Way We Were" and Elton John's "Bennie and the Jets" were the last two songs I remember hearing," she said before using her voice to sing "Ba Ba Ba Bennie and the Jets."

I see both Dave and Nathan's jaws drop as Aunt Wendy sings that particular phrase.

Dave says, "If your voice is that good, why don't you use it all the time? I can understand you clearly."

"This may be true," Aunt Wendy says, "But would you not agree that communication is a two way street? If I use my voice, people will not understand why I can't hear them. Some just think I can read lips as easily as I can speak. I can't read lips worth a dang. Yes, it helps to be post-lingually deaf to be able to read lips because you already have the puzzle in your head and you are just putting the puzzle together as you go. By puzzle, I mean the English language, one of the hardest languages to learn because of all the idioms involved. If you already have a good command of the English Language, it is easier to lipread. But lipreading is as much a talent as a skill. A study done in the 90's showed that college students…HEARING college students with no practice in lipreading did better than Deaf college students who had studied lipreading for years. I've met very few people who have this natural talent. One you know…Francis here."

"Francis?" the interpreters, Dave, and Nathan are confused for a minute.

"She refuses to call me Franz," Franz says while giving Aunt Wendy a mock stare.

Aunt Wendy gives Franz a mock stare right back and then continues with her story. "Frances," she took her time spelling out the whole name slowly, "is one of the best lipreaders I've ever met. She has a true gift made more amazing since she is pre-lingually Deaf, meaning she became Deaf before she acquired English."

Franz does several little bows to the people around the table. Eric, Rachel, and I give her a Deaf applause.

Aunt Wendy continues her story. "I went to a state residential school for the Deaf in Baltimore, Maryland, meaning I would live in a dorm on campus. It was a hard time for me….not being able to hear and not being able to sign. Being away from my family was devastating, but being with them was anguish because it reminded me that I was so different from them. My mom and dad never really got the hang of sign language. The only person who was there for me, who studied and signed with me every moment we were together was my little brother Gary – Elizabeth and Rachel's dad."

She pauses for a moment, seemingly lost in thought, before continuing. "I came home on weekends for a while. That's when Gary and I really bonded. The family went to sign language classes, but didn't really have time to learn. I felt as if I had lost my hearing and my family at the same time. I was one angry little girl, acting out and punching people when they didn't understand. Gary was my link to my family, but over the years, I spent less time with my natural family and more with my Deaf family. As soon as Gary was old enough to take the trains, he'd be with me on weekends. He became as fluent as I and was embraced by my friends at the Deaf school."

When Aunt Wendy shares about the closeness she felt with her signing brother, I look over at Nathan and wonder how this part impacts him. He's leaning forward, soaking in the story.

Aunt Wendy continues, "I graduated from the Maryland State School of the Deaf and went on to Gallaudet University in Washington DC. This is at the time Gallaudet was going through some changes. It was named Gallaudet College my first Prep year (Pre-Freshman) and then Gallaudet University the year I started my bachelors. By that time I was comfortable in my own skin. My ties with my family were almost nil except, of course, for Gary. I was fluent in ASL and feeling proud of my deafness. I know that sounds like a weird thing to say, but I felt more like someone from France who was bilingual, not like someone broken. When I talked to hearing people they would often say, 'Oh, I'm sorry.' I felt like saying, 'I'm not sorry at all. I'm doing great.' Others would say, 'Don't you miss sound?' and that's true. Since I grew up listening, there are some sounds I really miss. I just say, 'Yes, but I'm at peace, because my life is so rich.'

What bothers me the most is how hearing people feel a need to take care of us. Imagine you are at an all-boys college and the leadership feels that boys are way too violent to be good leaders, so the college is run by all females. There's a female president, female Board of Directors, female instructors. Maybe one male instructor is hired for sports. Haha. Imagine how that would feel at an all-boys college? Or that you are in an all-girls college and the administration feels as if girls are too emotional to be good leaders, so the whole thing is run by men. Male president, all the teachers are male, and there is an all-male Board of Directors."

Rachel taps on the table and I can feel the focus shift to her. "Imagine?" she signs. "It does not take much to imagine a girl's school run exclusively by males. You don't have to look back too many years."

There is general agreement around the circle, with nods and some signing, "True, true."

"Well, since Gallaudet was established," Aunt Wendy explains, "It has been run by hearing people. This practice continued even when there were skilled and qualified Deaf people around who could run it. The Board of Directors didn't really want all the power to be in Deaf people's hands, because they didn't feel that poor Deaf people could govern a college. It was insulting. Most of the people on our Board of Directors could not even sign. Some had never had a conversation with a Deaf person except through an interpreter.

"So that's the kind of atmosphere that existed at the college. There was an awakening for Deaf people and I was there to see it. It was an amazing time to be in college. Minorities were fighting for their civil rights and we wanted in on it. So, I was right in the middle of things in 1988, a year that means something to Deaf people. Gallaudet had already changed from a College to a University. But this is the year it became OUR University.

"The president retired and the Board looked for a new president. Since the Board of Directors was almost all hearing, they picked a hearing president who didn't even know sign. Can you imagine? She could not even talk with a Deaf person without an interpreter. She was possibly a good administrator, but we would have none of it. We wanted the president to go, and we wanted huge changes in the Board. We staged a college walkout, protests, and finally an all campus shutdown. Literally. We hotwired campus busses and parked them at the entrances and exits so no one could get in or out. We held signs that said 'Deaf President Now' which became DPN in shorthand. We were covered locally by the press, then throughout the USA, and finally the world.

"After several days we had a Deaf president. I feel a little bad for the woman the Board had picked, but she contacted the college and said she would not take the job with such unrest. She learned a lot about Deaf pride in those few days. The Board member ratio changed to where there were more Deaf people than hearing, which is how it should be. We specifically pressured some Board members to quit by revealing insulting things they had written about Deaf people.

"From that time on, Deaf people have been in charge of Gallaudet. I graduated with my Masters in teaching and got a job…here in Tandy with the State School for the Deaf."

A spontaneous Deaf applause breaks out around the table.

Aunt Wendy smiles and joins us in the applause before continuing. "Leaving a place with so many Deaf people and coming to Oregon was a cultural shock, but still worth it. Leaving my brother, who was now grown up and married, was the hardest part. His wife, Carla, didn't sign very much at all, but had a very good heart, and I knew she loved him. I headed out to Oregon and a steep learning curve. In 1997 my brother and his wife were expecting twins."

Everyone around the table is drinking in the story of this strong, adventurous, woman. I've heard the Gallaudet story more times than I can count, but love it every time. It is like history coming to life. My history.

Chapter 21

Aunt Wendy takes a minute to look at Rachel and me with such an expression of love.

She goes on to say, "We were over the moon about the news of the twins. We had graduated to email from an old fashioned technology, called a TTY device. Messages flew back and forth across the country. However, these two gals were a little too eager to get out into the world. They were born prematurely and could not breathe on their own sufficiently to oxygenate their little bodies. So they needed some support. The doctor assured Gary and Carla that a simple oxygen tent would be all they needed.

"The tent worked perfectly for Rachel, but there was a malfunction with the tent's oxygen sensor for Elizabeth and that change in oxygen was enough to damage her hearing. So the girls were identical, except for their hearing. Gary and Carla were stunned. Carla grieved the most, because she really didn't know me that well. Although she knew I was a professional, she could not shake the image of the person she once met on the subway begging for money and giving out alphabet cards.

"Doctors wondered at first if there was some kind of hereditary link, but with me being Deaf from meningitis and (after a full investigation) Elizabeth from the oxygen, it was just happenstance. After many long talks, Gary and Carla decided to move across the country and live in Tandy to be near me. Of course, I said no way, she laughs.

Rachel starts talking about our parents. "Dad is a well-known architect who can get jobs anywhere and is often flown across country to consult. He could get work on the North Pole," she grins. "Mom is a skilled nutritionist who hosts a very successful blog on nutrition and does one-on-one or group consultant work. Mom had already planned to do everything online once she had us, but she had not expected to have a crash course in ASL and Deaf culture."

"God bless her," Aunt Wendy joins in, "She was amazing. Carla not only took ASL classes at CCC, but she and Gary would do whole days of no voice, only sign language. Most of the time they used a mix of English and ASL, but in English order so they could talk and sign at the same time. They wanted to make sure both of their girls had a bilingual upbringing. When Elizabeth was four, she started doing pre-school at SSD where I worked. It was a blessing for me to be able to keep an eye out for her. A joy when I was able to babysit for the two of them."

"Love you, Aunt Wendy," I say. "But I fear if I don't stop you now our guests will learn about everything that happened from our first day until we entered Chenoa."

We all have a chuckle about that. Aunt Wendy accepts our teasing and then claps her hands as if a queen ordering servants. She orders Rachel and me into the kitchen to bring out the dessert.

"Oh, I'll help," Dave says as he shoots up from his chair.

I sit down and gesture for him to follow my sister. He blushes all the way to the kitchen. A few minutes later they come out with pieces of pumpkin pie topped with whipped cream. Another Deaf applause from the table. Once we're all seated I ask Dave if he has heard anything more about the scamming siblings.

He shakes his head in dismay and says, "The police kept us updated while they thought Steve was still in the area. Stacie Wallace is set to be sentenced in the next two weeks. The police think the judge will go easy on her because she gave us the info on her brother. She could have gotten up to five years in jail. Now it looks like it will be probation or no more than three years. Really, we don't know what the judge will do. It's not a jury and we don't have access to any of Stacie's previous deeds or misdeeds."

Eric asks, "Why do the police think Steve's no longer in the area?"

"Well," Dave explains, "They have kept it out of the papers that Stacie is in custody. The police think Steve is still waiting for her in Vegas. I don't know why because she won't be coming with any money."

Nathan says, "I was impressed to see Elizabeth fly into action when the campus was locked down. But it is beyond me that you four got out of that locked office. I'm afraid I would have just stayed there until someone came to find me."

"Thank goodness for those fingernail clippers that Eric found," I reply, "Or we might have been in there for a long time."

"And none of that would have been possible had it not been for ninja girl over here," Eric smiles. "That jerk zip-tied us with our arms behind our back. Francis..." he smiled, using her full name, "...stepped right through the zip-tie and suddenly her hands were in front. Impressive."

"If you are ever in that situation again, there are a few things you can do with zip-ties. I'm not a police officer, but had to go through self-defense classes before getting my security guard certification. CCC requires all guards to have them," Dave explains. He looks around and sees that he has everyone's attention so he continues. "If your kidnapper is not very knowledgeable, and you have decided you cannot beat him, then present your own hands to be zip-tied. Don't let him or her make the decision for you. Cross your wrists and flex your hands very tightly. He'll put the zip-tie on and make it tight. Don't try to be brave but really play up how tight it is and how much it hurts. Don't move your hands from that position until he is gone.

Then by moving your hands from crossed fists to limp palms together, you can slip out of almost any zip-tie. This is for front or back. If your hands are crushed together palm to palm you won't have wiggle room, but you can still break the zip-tie by putting your arms over your head and bringing them down past your chest."

We encourage him to demonstrate, so although a blush starts creeping up from below his collar, he dutifully stands and shows us the routine. Aunt Wendy puts a finger in the air meaning, one moment, and disappears into the kitchen. She returns with a zip-tie. We all cheer – Deaf applause. She goes right up to him, shows him the way she wants him to place his hands together and zip-ties him. She backs up and there he is, in full blush, ready to demonstrate. He raises his hands over his head and then comes down against his chest and his elbows carry-through. It happens so fast, we don't even see the zip-tie flying. Deaf applause.

I look over and see my sister, a big goofy smile on her face. I can tell she really likes this guy. I'm very happy for her. I look at Nathan and Eric, both really neat guys. I just could not decide, nor should I have to. I will become a vet. I will become a vet. I almost laugh at my mantra.

We all help clear the table after the zip-tie demonstration. Full of dinner and pie, we're comfortable. I see Franz and Barbara talking about school and such over in the corner. I see Aunt Wendy discretely hand each interpreter an envelope. Rachel asks if any help is needed, but her eyes are pleading that she be allowed to beg off to go with Dave. "He wants to show me a couple of houses. He's thinking of buying his own place. He's looking for a little fixer-upper and then plans to work on it for a few years. After that he'll trade up. Isn't that brilliant?" she signs, eyes glowing.

"We have everything handled here," I sign to her and add, "Stay safe," and wiggle my eyebrows up and down. Rachel squints at me, then blooms into a big smile and mouths, "Thank you."

I watch them leave. Barbara says she will give Franz a ride…Hmmm. Everyone leaves except Nathan and Eric, awkwardly signing to each other in the living room. They are doing a battle of who gets to stay longer. Oh, no. I want none of that.

I walk into the living room and gesture that they can leave. I feel like a dang mime. Why is this happening to me? "Thank you." I know Nathan knows that. I gesture coming here. I point at my wrist and tap at an invisible watch. "Bye." I then gesture that I'm going back in to help Aunt Wendy wash dishes. "Bye, thank you." Then I walk over and open the door for them.

Nathan gives me a hug and leaves, taking each step down the porch slowly. He's making sure Eric is coming, too. Eric gives me a hug and then signs to me "Wow, you could be a professional mime. What a skill."

I slap his arm and he chuckles as he strides down the stairs.

I close the door and slump into the nearest chair. Aunt Wendy comes in, sees me, and just laughs. "Stop it," I tell her. "It's not funny." Then we just smile at each other.

"Thank you so much for hosting the party," I tell her, "I know you paid for the interpreters and everything. Plus you work tomorrow. I know you did it for us, our hearing friends who don't know ASL. Can I help pay…"

I only get that part out and there is a storm in Aunt Wendy's eyes. "Don't you dare," she says. "You are my nieces and I enjoy every minute with you. Come on. You know me better than that. If I didn't want to do this I wouldn't have. And I was able to share my Gallaudet story. How many times have you heard that story? And you didn't run screaming from the dining room. True family love, that's what I call it."

I get on my coat and head for the car. On the way home I feel so lucky to have so much in my life.

Rachel gets home super late and floats past me to her bedroom. "Did you use protection, young lady," I sign sternly.

"Oh shut up," she smiles. "We're not there yet…"

"Oh, y-e-t," I show emphasis by spelling out the word 'yet.'

"I really like him," Rachel says. "But sometimes he's hard to get to know. He does this pull – push thing with me that drives me crazy. His parents divorced when he was 12 so every time he gets close emotionally, he gets scared and starts pushing me away. I have not even met his mom or dad. So, I'm not picking out any wedding invitations. Also, you know my rule. Before anyone joins the family, they have to know ASL."

"That's a pretty powerful rule," I say, flattered.

"Well…," Rachel draws out the sign, "When it comes to Dave, maybe I'll say, he has to be pretty good at ASL. Not fluent."

I throw a pillow at her.

Chapter 22

"I think when he starts taking ASL, that will show he wants to be part of my life. Right now, we're just enjoying each other," Rachel says.

"What do you think of dating a Deaf guy?" I ask.

"Well, that was random. Depends on the Deaf guy," Rachel says. "I don't have any rules against that. I mean, I'm already part of the culture, so it would not be a culture shock. Why are you asking?"

"You know I'm dating Nathan and Eric," I say, almost talking to myself.

"I heard something about that," Rachel replies.

I heave another pillow her way.

"I'm a little confused," I try to explain my feelings. "I'm not against hearing people. It's just that I think communication is such an important part of a serious relationship. When Nathan and I are texting back and forth, he's a dream. He's funny, playful, thoughtful, natural. When he's with me, other than sports or kissing….when it comes to communicating, it's almost painful. Then there's Eric. I love him. But do I love him like a friend or more than that? I don't know. I have a lot of fun with Nathan, but I have fun with Eric, too. But, I'm afraid if I let myself be in love with Eric, he'll be picking out wedding invitations. I'm not ready for that."

"Good questions, all," Rachel responds, and we both smile. "But tomorrow is a school day, so I'm going to let you dream the answer. I already know what I'm going to dream about."

"If it's that kind of dream, you better take protection," I tease. Suddenly I see two pillows flying in my direction.

*

Thursday flies by and I do an extra-long run which exhausts me yet clears my head. For the first few miles, as is my habit, I memorize biology vocabulary. Each landing of my foot on the sidewalk pounds the spelling and meaning into my brain. I keep two lists in my mind….one on the right and one on the left. The right side holds all the vocabulary I'm confident of and the left…those words I keep tripping over. Each time I run, I pull the words from the left side to the right. I even write my notes that way, so I could SEE them while I run.

I keep my eyes alert on the roads for any driver not paying attention. I know reflecting strips on my clothes are not what the 'cool kids' are wearing these days but I wear them, but I wear them anyway. I have to chuckle to myself. In this way I'm like Aunt Wendy. I don't care about my running outfit except that it is visible to traffic. If that means wearing an orange cone on my head, so be it. I laugh. Okay, no orange cone, but I do go for reflecting strips. When I'm running on the streets, I care about safety, especially when the gray skies of November can make it seem like night at 3:30 in the afternoon. By the time I hit the Junior High near my house, I'm in phase two. This is the mind-clearing part. I let my brain go blank and just run. I almost always have an empty track, so different from a road full of cars, bikes, or other vehicles. On the track I don't have to be hyper-vigilant to make sure no one is coming.

My glide goes from a jog to a smooth run. I can feel my muscles stretch out, and soon it's just me, pushing against the wind. The rhythm is like music, at least my kind of music, and I feel I can do this for days. Of course, after a while I go back to jogging and head home. The last couple of blocks I slow down to a walk and even out my strides. I end my run feeling taller than when I started because my muscles feel as if they have been stretched to their limit.

I grab a big glass of water and finish it in front of the sink. The next fill-up goes downstairs with me. Although I get my biology midterm results tomorrow, I know I did well. I didn't look at any question and think…What the heck is that? I wonder how Nathan did? No midterm or final for math, just five packets, five tests. With the last test, the class is complete. It's individualized but with a teacher for questions in the Math Lab. As long as I don't fall behind, it's pretty straight-forward. I hate taking math in classrooms where the teacher can't sign because I can never follow the instructor writing on the board and the interpreter at the same time. Lag time. Often the interpreter doesn't know what is going on so has to keep looking at the board. It's a mess. So an independent math study is perfect for me.

Reading is okay. What is really helpful about the reading class is that it is half reading and half study skills. So, much of my reading class I'm actually using for biology.

After a shower, I settle down for some studying. Of course that's the exact time my texts blow up. Franz needs a little help with one of the reading questions, Eric wants a date on Saturday night, and Nathan wants a date Friday. Eric is taking me to our favorite hamburger place in all of Tandy. Actually, it's a mini-chain, Tommy's Burgers, that serve better burgers than you can make a home. At least better than I can make at home. Their fries, always fresh, are served in brown paper bags. I can almost taste them.

Nathan has something in mind, he said mysteriously, but won't tell me. He only says to wear a dress. Hmmm…sounds fancy. I'm not quite the fancy type, but always look forward to an adventure. Even after Wednesday night, and the jealous looks they exchanged between them, both Nathan and Eric want to date me. Am I a bad person? No. I've been honest with them both. End of story. (I AM going to be a vet.)

I answer yes to both Eric and Nathan. I then text Franz, which turns into facetime as we go through the questions from our reading. Once done, I turn off the alerts and dig into my homework.

Rachel comes home late again. Not exactly floating on air this time, since Dave is starting to push her away. She brought up visiting his college and meeting his dad. I guess it is too soon because he doesn't ask her out for Friday or Saturday night. He stops talking about the house he wants to buy and fix up. Trouble in paradise? Hope not. She is crushing pretty bad.

I see her in her bedroom, sitting cross legged, her journal open, writing her heart on the page. After that big fight when we were younger and I snooped, I have never opened those journals again. I know it would be going too far.

Friday is one of those days that anger Tandyites. It can be beautiful weather Monday through Thursday and then turn dreary for the weekend. Grrrrrr. It is dark and rainy when Rachel and I drive to Chenoa in the morning. We stop in Building 2 by the Food Station and stand in line at the coffee area. With mochas in hand, we head off in different directions for our day. We'll meet back after Rachel's last class.

I aced my biology midterm. Yay!! Yes, it was a low A, but an A nonetheless. With the extra credit it lifts my last B to an A, so I have an A going into the final. Yay. Nathan shows his A, the smarty pants, and does the Deaf applause for mine.

He also signs, "Saturday night, you me, dancing?"

What? He's taking me dancing? And he signs the whole thing. No wonder he would not tell me. He wanted to show me his signing. Yay, team Nathan!

I meet Franz for lunch. We chat for a while about the Wednesday dinner. She loves my Aunt Wendy and says again how lucky I am to have her in my life. I ask about Robert, since I have not heard about Franz's brother lately. He is a lot older than she is, so they are not close. He no longer lives at home and is not very good at signing. Franz says that he is hooked up with a gallery at the coast and is selling his welding sculptures. He makes these amazing garden sculptures that move with the wind. He is now working with a start-up company on how the sculpture can be set on a foundation that can send a current to the homeowner. It would not only be beautiful, but make electricity…like an exquisite windmill. He calls it 'Green Art.' He and the start-up techs calculate that the whole set up could be paid off in five years, allowing the home owner to have free electricity after that. Not enough electricity to make their whole bill free, but to save money every month. Pretty nifty. Franz is very proud of her big brother but mourns a relationship that could have been if only he had learned ASL. Franz's parents are the same way. She was often in the dark as to what is going on because they never really learned her language. When she came out to them, she had to bring an interpreter. I cannot imagine.

I drop my hands to a lower level, private signing, and asked about her leaving with Barbara. I wiggled my eyebrows. Franz is very private and just smiled and signed, "We'll see."

"Did she ask you out? Did you ask her out? Did you set up another time to meet?" I ask, firing question marks with one hand after the other like a gunslinger.

She gives me this serious glare, then rolls her eyes. "Let me give you the definition of 'let's see.'"

I give her a minute more to decide if she wants to say more.

"Okay, we're going to Portland to some event. Barbara lives in Portland, so we're going to have dinner and just hang out a little. As F-R-I-E-N-D-S," she spells slowly.

"Ah… 'the lady doth protest too much,'" I sign and smile.

"What the heck does that mean?" Franz signs.

"Shakespeare's Hamlet," I say, "It means that you are emphasizing that you two are friends. You are going out of your way to be casual about the whole thing." I give her a big grin. "You like her! It's like a Freshman ark. We're all pairing up two by two."

"Only if it is a very liberal Bible," Franz rolls her eyes at my comment. "Two by two was male and female. Dave and Rachel could get on board but I don't think Barbara and I would make the cut, not to mention you and two guys! That's not the story I read."

We both laugh and I have to admit she is right. I don't see Eric at lunch and wonder if he is just busy or not wanting to be seen as the same 'old friend' that I usually have lunch with.

Math is going well. I made sure I'm half a packet ahead so I can be done a week before the end of the term. Then I can spend all my time working on reading and biology. Fitness is a breeze, since I only have to log my running.

Eric is there in reading with a warm smile. He looks a bit tidier than his usual college look. If he is trying to impress me, he is doing a pretty good job. We chat a little before class, but as soon as class begins, my eyes are on the interpreter. This class needs focus. About half way through class I feel my phone vibrate, but don't check on it. Whoever it is can wait until after class, which is in about 30 more minutes.

Once class is over, I look down and see it's from Rachel texting, "Dave is going to pick me up after class so the car is all yours."

"I've got the car," I signed to Eric, who was waiting for me. "Rachel is going somewhere with Dave." I'm crossing my fingers for Rachel and Dave.

"Nice," Eric says, "I sure like him, or rather I like the way he treats Rachel."

I nod in agreement.

"Want to start our date early? It's 3:30 and we could catch a movie before Tommy's. Those hamburgers are calling me," he smiles.

"Thanks," I reply, "But I have some things to do, and I don't always get the car all to myself. Do you want to meet there or are we car-pooling?"

"I'm picking you up at 6:00 PM. This is not a gathering; it is a date," he signs with a confidence I don't usually see from him. He leans over and gives me a peck on the lips. Just the right amount of pressure to let me know that he is not my little buddy. Oh my, how right he is. Yay, team Eric.

By the time I had finished my first chore, new fingernail polish from Walgreens, I receive another message from Rachel. "Dave has a surprise. You won't believe it. Come to 2240 Claude St. SE NOW!"

I remember Rachel said Dave was looking for a house to fix up and then flip.

"On my way," I text back and receive a big smile emoji for my prompt response.

I make my way over past the post office to Claude St. It is an older neighborhood of 1940's and 50's houses, one to three bedrooms, one car garages. A little uneven for an investment because some of the yards are well kept up, but others look rather shabby. I find the right address which has a 'For Sale' sign out front. As I drive by the garage door opens and is empty. I look for Dave's car. Probably hiding somewhere. I roll my eyes. Just like my sister to have the artistic 'reveal.'

I park inside the garage and see a sign on the inside door, "Enter by the front door."

Oh, Sis, I smile to myself. You really are loving this. The lawn is well manicured and there are azaleas on each side of the porch. A maple out in front has dropped most of its leaves, which I'm sure have been vacuumed up by some company that takes care to note curb appeal when selling a home. Next to the doorbell was a little sign which reads, "Come in and make yourself at home. Dave and Rachel."

My hand freezes at the doorknob. Did Dave propose? So soon! Did my level-headed sister accept? She was just saying that she hadn't even met the parents yet. I place a big smile on my face and enter the love nest.

My mouth gapes. I see my sister tied to a chair, tears running down her face. Her hands are zip-tied. Her shoulders and legs are bound by rope.

Chapter 23

My mind can't seem to process the information. Nothing makes sense. I look into the eyes of my sister who looks paler than I've ever seen her. She suddenly jerks her body; her eyes enlarge with terror. I spin around and am face to face with a stranger. But, he's not a stranger. For a moment I don't even recognize him. His blonde hair is black, and his once clean-shaven face has a three week old beard, darkened as well. It's Steven Wallace. Even his sister, Stacie, would not have recognized him on the street. He stands there with a smirk on his face. In one hand he holds a gun, and in the other, a pair of scissors.

Wallace gestures with the gun for me to sit in the chair near my sister. I back up carefully, shaking to my bones, and sit. He makes a big production of using the scissors to cut through my sister's zip-tie, keeping his gaze and gun on me.

She begins to sign, stiffly. "Tell her what I say and use your mouth while you do it so you can't trick me. Make it clear." She's interpreting his words. "You two cheated me out of a half million dollars after I had to spend months in that crap job as a rent-a-cop. Stacie and I had it all figured out and would be long gone if it weren't for you. So you two are going to help me get back my half million and my sister. Are you hurt? NO. Is your sister hurt? NO. Do you want it to stay that way? YES. I have not hurt anyone yet, but I will to get my sister back, do you hear me or see me or whatever?"

I nod, and feel numb. He directs Rachel to tell me to put my wrists out for the zip-tie. Next he ties me to the back of the chair, then my legs to the legs of the chair. Rachel and I. Twins. Bound bookends. I can't believe this is happening.

He starts pacing around and keeps talking. He takes out his gun and points it at each of us in turn. "You two are going to help me, and if you are good little girls, I will not have to hurt you. People will kill for half a million. But that's not my style. I will make sure you are safe when my sister is free and we're gone with the money. Are you going to run away? NO. Do you want to stay alive? YES."

Before he zip-ties her hands again, he thinks of something else. "You may think your cell phone beacon is working when people discover that you are missing, but the phones are in the freezer, which means they can't be traced. I could have put them in the blender, but as you can tell with your sister, her phone comes in very handy, doesn't it." He ends his conversation by shaking two sets of keys in our faces….our keys, and then stuffing them in his pockets.

My sister is mouthing and signing and crying all at the same time. She feels bad that it was her phone that brought me to the house. But I mouth, it's okay, it's okay, it's okay over and over until she nods.

Steve zip-ties my sister's hands and I notice she clenches her fists and crosses them at the wrist, the way Dave showed us at Aunt Wendy's party. He pulls the zip tightly and she looks like she cries out in pain because he puts his head to hers and talks very fast. She nods and puts her hands in her lap.

I move my hands around the best I can and tap my finger towards my wrist and mouth "time."

Rachel shrugs; then opens one fist to make the number eight. Good, that means Eric is at the house wondering where I am. Even if we were not dating, I would never stand him up and he knows it. He'll be worried and so will my parents. They'll check my cell phone and not understand why I'm not answering…unless, oh my gosh, what if Steve Wallace is answering for us, saying we are detained. He has our phones. He can answer for both of us.

Steve Wallace comes back into the room with a newspaper and a cell phone. I can tell by the case it is not Rachel's or mine. He pulls the chairs closer together, throwing us both off balance, and tosses the newspaper in our laps. He then takes a picture and leaves with the phone. I can just imagine the caption 'Twins Kidnapped." He wants his sister to be released with a half million dollars. This will terrify our family. How are they expected to get their hands on that kind of money. It's a Friday night and the banks are closed anyway.

Rachel straightens up. She opens then closes her palms, thumbs touching, to indicate the door shutting. He's leaving? What is going on? We wonder if we should make a break for it. He could be outside. We look around for whatever we can find that could be used as a weapon. The place is pretty bare except what Wallace brought for his plan: a card table, three chairs, a lamp, a sleeping bag, and some wrappers in a trash can.

We don't even sign for fear he is just testing us and is watching us from some curtain he left open in the kitchen. I can tell when Rachel moves her head in a certain way, she is listening. In comes Wallace with a big smile on his face, carrying a tray of sodas and a bag from some fast food chain. He says something to the two of us, but I have no idea what it is. Rachel lifts her hands as if she cannot sign in that restrained position and Wallace rolls his eyes.

He tests the ropes that tie our chests to the chairs and the ones that tie our legs. He then pushes the card table towards us and places food on top. The last thing he does is cut our zip-ties.

"Let the games begin," Wallace says. "Your parents, the police, and the head of the Chenoa Foundation will be getting their messages about now. If the college does not answer on the weekend, so much the sadder for you two. You will be my guests for a while. Hope the time does not run out. Boo-hoo." We can see he is very proud of himself.

He pushes the food towards us. "EAT! No one is going to be able to say I didn't treat you well. This is good food. So don't get me mad. Just eat." He slams his hand on the table and I can feel it vibrate all the way through my body.

We begin to eat and his mood gets cheerier. Rachel signs and asks to be able to talk to me.

"Oh, yeah," he says, "Tell her how I tricked you. That was the best part, the most dangerous part. Tell her," he points his half eaten hamburger in my direction. "Don't try anything sneaky. Talk when you sign."

Rachel begins, "I was in Drawing class and got a note from security that someone had scratched the car and the person was really sorry."

"I added that really sorry part." Wallace interrupted. "The gal at the Security Office window ate that up. I looked so sad," he mocks a sad face as he chews.

Rachel continues, "So I go out to the car to check it out. I see a paper under the windshield wiper. As I'm getting the note off, Wallace comes up behind me with a gun."

"Does she like my new do?" Wallace says, pointing to his hair and beard, "I think she does. It took her a while to recognize me. I saw when it happened because her eyes got really big."

I can tell that he's having a good time mocking us and reliving the capture. He continues the story, "I had a car just two slots down and we get in real easy like. I already had this sweet place picked out. Once we were rolling, I just had to keep my fingers crossed that no one would notice us. Once inside, the rest was easy. I got your sister's phone. I go to text you. I have this great idea about your sister wanting to get a place with you. But while I'm looking in messages I see the name 'Dave' and recognize his number. Perfect. That idiot Dave was always saying how he wanted to get a house someday and fix it all up. What a chump. I contacted you both times with Rachel's phone and we just waited for you to get here."

The hamburger tastes like sawdust in my mouth. I take a tiny sip from the soda and then push the food away from me. Rachel does the same. As soon as our food is pushed away he zip-ties us again. We sit there for about 20-30 minutes in silence when Rachel tells Wallace that she has to go to the bathroom. I catch the word bathroom and nod to Wallace that I have to go as well.

He snips Rachel's zip-tie with his scissors and starts talking. "I planned that out as well," he said. "You know I only need one of you for my plan to work. So if you go to the bathroom and try to do anything sneaky, I shoot your sister." With that he walks over and picks up a pillow. He can see I'm confused. He talks to Rachel.

"It's called the poor man's silencer." she signed.

He cuts me out of the zip-tie and unties my legs and shoulders. Then he points the pillow at my sister and I find the bathroom. I look quickly around for some kind of weapon. It's an empty house to begin with and all that's there is a roll of tissue paper and a dirty bar of soap. I complete my business and get back to the living room. He then directs me to untie Rachel. Once she's untied he uses the scissors to cut the zip-tie and has my sister tie me up, body, and both legs. He points the gun at me and with a wicked smile, gives Rachel a little wave. When Rachel disappears, he puts down the gun long enough to zip-tie my hands. This time I use the fist to fist technique Dave showed us. He zips and I wince as the plastic digs into my skin. Upon Rachel's return, he ties her in the chair, but does not zip-tie her wrists.

He's pretty familiar with the interpreting process by watching us so closely, so he just starts talking. "The police have the biggest decision to make. I'm sure your mom and dad can figure out how to get their hands on a half million. But I'm not going without Stacie, so they have to know I'm serious. I want her to be taken to the airport and left with the suitcase of money and a small plane filled with gas. I can fly the plane. I'll fly low to skip all the radar. We'll be off and once we're far away, I'll radio where you two lovelies are. So, make yourself as comfortable as possible, it's going to be a long night."

With that, he zip-ties Rachel's hands, hits the light, and gets in his sleeping bag. He rolls the scissors and gun in his jacket and puts it behind his head. He just stares at us. After a few minutes he gets up and fetches our coats and drapes them over our shoulders for a little extra warmth since there is none in the house. I'm guessing he will be staying up all night. I was thankful that he left the bathroom light on. Of course he did it so he could see us in the night, but I don't know if I could handle total darkness which would make me dizzy. Rachel and I look at each other.

She mouths, "I love you."

I mouth back, "I love you, too."

I plan scenarios in my head until I fall asleep, my head bent down with my chin touching my chest.

Chapter 24

Rachel and I wake up with our necks hurting and a little light filtering in between the shades. We look around and realize that Wallace left sometime early in the morning. We don't know when he'll be coming back, but we imagine he went out for a newspaper and breakfast. I sign as tiny as I can, in case he is testing us again. I don't want to make him mad.

"Nothing in the bathroom," I sign.

"I looked, too," Rachel signs. "He only unties us one at a time when we go to the bathroom."

"He'll probably do the same thing with the newspaper to show 'proof of life' and then untie us for the bathroom," I said and Rachel nodded, ever so slightly. "I don't trust that he will leave us alive."

Rachel nods again and signs, "If we could get to the lamp, maybe we can bash him. Can you get out of your zips?"

"I think so," I tell her.

"I practiced last night when he was snoring and I can get out of the zip-ties, but not this rope. Keep alert and we'll look for a chance to use that lamp. He is not saving zip-ties, so I'm sure he has plenty somewhere," Rachel says, then stiffens. I know Wallace has returned.

Wallace blusters in with a newspaper, throws it on us, and takes a picture. He rushes out to send another message to whomever. He has some water, coffee, and a bag of donuts. With all this, I'm convinced he has a car hidden somewhere down the street. Maybe he changes where he parks it each time so he doesn't attract attention. He does not even warn us this time, just cuts the zip-ties with his scissors.

My sister says she has to go to the bathroom. I nod that I have to go as well.

"Of course you do," he smirks.

My sister reaches for the newspaper and starts reading about us being kidnapped. There is a picture of the two of us and Wallace on the front page. My sister squints at the print and asks, "So they agreed? How do you know?" She is trying to look fascinated and confused at the same time. I know that look and understand something is going to happen.

We watch Wallace go over and pick up the lamp and put it on the table so we can read about his brilliance. I think…game on.

"I really have to go to the bathroom," I sign and Rachel voices my concern.

Then Rachel starts talking and signing, "Look at that! They have the old picture of Wallace! Oh, no, not even his sister would recognize him now. That's how he's been able to go in and out of the house without anyone even suspecting."

I can see all this praise is having an effect on Wallace, because he's grinning and nodding and saying things, "Yup," or "Oh, yes," (I can only assume) and begins untying me, breaking with his usual routine. Once my upper body is free, he bends down and begins to undo my right leg, listening the whole time to my sister's voice telling him how amazing he is.

"Rachel and Elizabeth Carn," she's reading the newspaper now, "went missing from Chenoa Community College yesterday and are assumed kidnapped by Steve Wallace pictured above."

His back is to Rachel and so when she says "pictured above" she adds the 'coffee' sign. I get it immediately. As she is reading she is smoothing the paper of the front page with her right hand inching towards the lamp.

I grab the two coffees and throw them at Wallace's face squishing the lids off while aiming the hot liquid into his eyes. He screams words I can only imagine are profanity while my sister grabs the top of the lamp and swings the base directly at his head.

His head freezes in midair, exactly how I've seen it in a hundred cartoons, and then in slow motion he falls to the ground.

Rachel and I look at each other, eyes wide. We did it. But before any celebrating, we get to work. I finish untying my legs, then put his arms behind his back and securely wrap his hands. Only then do I untie Rachel's shoulders which are still pressed against the high back chair. I go back to working on Wallace as she unties her legs. We're both stiff from being restrained for more than 18 hours. But the adrenaline has kicked in and we're going fast. I get the scissors from his back pocket and the gun from his jacket.

Rachel, now free, does one of the sweetest things I've ever seen. She checks his pulse. Here this guy kidnapped us TWICE, threatened us and our friends, and probably planned on leaving us for dead. Yet my sister thinks to check for a pulse. I look into that face, which is mine, and she nods. I feel my eyes start to fill and shake it off. Now is not the time. I can hug her later. Yes, we have a 'later' once we get this jerk sewn up like a goose.

I zip-tie his ankles. We both go through pockets in his jeans and jacket finding matches, our keys, zip-ties, a pocket knife, his cell and what looks like his own car keys. Together we open the sleeping bag zipper all the way and pat it down to make sure nothing is hidden inside. We move the chairs and table away and push the bag near his body. We then roll him into the sleeping bag and zip him up. Then starting from the feet up, we crisscross the rope all the way to his neck. When he wakes up, he will be in a straitjacket.

We each use the bathroom. Funny, in all those TV shows about people being kidnapped, they never show the rescued person saying, "Excuse me, I need to go to the bathroom." It dawns on me why and

I shudder. We're two very lucky sisters.

We then retrieve our phones. Dead, ruined, or not working. How do we get help? We can't leave him here because he might die, or worse, get out.

I tell Rachel to go ahead to the police and I will stay with Wallace to make sure he doesn't escape. She refuses. If he gets out I will be his hostage all over again. If we both leave in the car, he might get out.

"You are the runner. You could get to the post office in five minutes." Rachel says.

"No, let's stay close. There has to be neighbors or something. I mean, it's light outside," I counter.

I nod and go over to open the front door. Life, traffic, kids playing, I would bet there are cell phones everywhere. I point to the newspaper and share my plan. This time Rachel agrees. She grabs the paper and runs outside, looking back to make sure she can still see me. I'm watching her and at the same time holding the lamp. The next time it can be my pleasure to knock out Wallace.

I watch her cup her hands to the side of her mouth and yell in both directions. She boldly steps into the middle of the road with the newspaper held out at arm's length. Someone pulls over and I can see her pointing to her face, the newspaper and the house. I glance back to Wallace and can see he is coming to….confused and hurting. He can't move and can't see that well. He still has coffee in his eyes. I don't care. Outside, the driver, bless her heart, is talking on the phone. Rachel looks at me and signs 911 'thumb up', letting me know the woman is calling the police.

Wallace is starting to move in ways that would make a hip hop dancer proud. I'm sure he's screaming vile things at me. Tra la. I just point to my ear and shrug my shoulders. Rachel is now talking on the phone by the lady's car.

Rachel comes back in and signs that the police are on their way. They promise to call our parents who will get the word out that we're safe. She looks at Wallace who is red faced, mouthing obscenities, and worming his way around the room. She signs to me that he is asking what is going on. But as Rachel is no longer moving her lips, he is clueless.

Since our faces are plastered across the morning newspaper, I'm hoping police arrive quickly. As soon as the thought crosses my mind I see that slight head tilt which tells me Rachel hears something. She makes the sign for sirens.

We wave from the front door as four, wow, four squad cars arrive, blocking off the street and in front of the house. The first two officers enter the open door with guns raised until they see our criminal tied up in a sleeping bag. They can't help but laugh. Rachel asks one of the police something and he gives her a wink, pulls out his cell and snaps a picture of Wallace in our handiwork.

We're almost giddy with relief. The police communicate with the other officers. Wallace is not escaping this time. Two additional officers come into the house and have the same reaction when they see Wallace. We show them the cells (which are still dead) defrosting in the kitchen as well as the gun and scissors on the table. We hand over his keys, cell, and other things he had with him.

Two officers leave with Wallace's keys. One of the two has an official looking camera and begins taking pictures of everything. The officer with the camera and her partner take us to a different room and take pictures of the welts on our wrists where the zip-ties dug into the skin. They also check our back, chest, and ankles for bruises or traction burns where the ropes secured us to the chair. They ask if we need further medical support and if we're on medications that are needed. We're fine; just need to see our family.

"I thought our parents would be here," I sign and Rachel voices to one of the officers.

One of the officers explains, "As far as we know, this is still a dangerous area. Your parents are waiting for you down at the precinct. Trust me, there are plenty of other folks there as well. It looks like some kind of homecoming. But, we need to debrief you while everything is fresh in your minds. And sorry, I know you are very close, but we have to do so separately. We have already sent for an interpreter who will be working with you, Ms. Carn. It won't take too long before you will be able to see your welcome home party."

The two officers inside are still taking photos while the first two officers, Rachel, and I leave by the front door.

"My name is Officer Baker. You'll be coming with me, Ms. Carn, while your sister will be going with Officer Hernandez." Rachel signs for me, then turns to the officers, "What about our car and our keys?"

"Someone will be by to pick them up later once all the photos have been taken," the officer smiles. "We'll take good care of them."

We both nod and go to our respective squad cars. After I get in the back seat, which is really creepy since there are no door handles on the inside, Officer Baker on the passenger side signs to me. She signs, "You're safe here."

I don't know if she meant I'm safe here in the car, or if she means 'now' since she kind of put two signs together, but I'm touched that she attempts to sign to me. I respond by signing "Thank you," and I can see she is relieved that the communication went smoothly.

Rachel and I are both brought into the precinct by the back door and are lead to different bathrooms. There I was given a little box filled with a comb, soap, tiny toothbrush, and towel. There is also a bottle of water. Heaven. Officer Baker writes on a piece of paper, "Do you need a rape kit?" My head jerks back and I shake my head 'no' but I start crying. This could have been so much worse. I use the little box of supplies but find my hands are shaking. The officer pats my shoulder and then steps back. She has to stay with me, but is trying to give me a little privacy through distance. Once I start cleaning off all the grime, I start to feel better. Little by little.

I'm lead into a room with a table and two chairs…as sparse as the living room I just left. Hey, I'm safe, I say to myself. Why does everything suddenly make me cry?

Chapter 25

In walks an officer followed by Sara from Chenoa. I get up and hug her. We sit and the questions begin. I re-tell everything to the best of my ability from the first phone call from Rachel's phone on campus to Rachel stopping someone in the street. Once the interview is over someone comes in with my cell. First, my phone has to be dusted for fingerprints before it can be fixed. I open the phone and can't even count the number of texts I have.

"I have a few questions of my own," I ask the detective through Sara. "Has Steve Wallace been charged?"

"Indeed," the officer replies. "Because of the fine work you and your sister did, he's looking at falsifying records, embezzlement, multiple counts of kidnapping, reckless endangerment, extortion, and...," the officer smiles, "impersonating a burrito."

It takes me a minute to get that last one, but when I do, I laugh. Oh, it feels good to laugh.

"Rachel hit him pretty hard and I threw scalding coffee in his eyes. Are we in trouble in any way since it was self-defense?" I ask.

"No, it was clearly self-defense. He took pictures of you tied and zip-tied so he can't yell 'victim' at any time," the officer responds.

"Last question," I say then add, "For now." The officer smiles as

I continue. "What happened to Stacie Wallace? Oh, who got the ransom money together?

"Last question?" the officer's eyes twinkle. "Okay. Your parents were in the process of collecting the money. I don't know how. You will have to ask them about that. We did have a plane with some gas in it, but not enough to leave the USA. We fixed the dial so it would read 'full.' About Stacie…and how she gave up her brother to save herself? That was a ruse. They had a plan that if something went wrong, the one caught would tell a story about the other going to Vegas. By the way, Steve Wallace can't fly a plane to save his hide. It is Stacie who is the pilot. We started to put two and two together when he made his demands. Is that your final question?"

I nod and sign, "Thank you." We leave the room and are guided to one heck of a family reunion. Everyone is in the hallway, including Rachel, who has just left the other interview room a few minutes earlier.

Deaf applause.

It is a whirl of faces; and frankly, I do not understand why I keep tearing up. I'm sure it is just the total relief of the whole thing being over. I go around the group, hugging and laughing. Franz will never talk to me again if I don't bring her on the next adventure. Mom and Dad, both looking as if they have had no sleep, crush Rachel and me in their arms. We stand there like a four legged stool for a while. When we release I ask them how they got the money together.

They say that the banks would not open, so Nathan, they point in his direction and he looks down at his feet knowing they were talking about him, convinced his dad to pull some strings. I suspect his father did more than that, since the bankers were even willing to talk to us.

"We were in negotiation when we got word from the police you had escaped. Escaped!" My mom starts crying again. "Those pictures of my babies tied up…"

I give her a little squeeze and go over to Nathan. I give him a hug and look for my sister, who understands and comes over as well.

"I hear you convinced your dad to help our parents with the money side. Thank you so much. We're both in his debt. Please send him our deepest 'thank you,'" I sign and Rachel translates.

"So no dancing tonight?" Nathan asks, that sweet twinkle in his eye.

"Sleeping for tonight," I answer. "Sleeping for the rest of the weekend!"

"Okay," he smiles, "But I'm not sure I'm ready for that kind of commitment in our relationship." He wiggles his eyebrows.

Rachel signs, "Oooookaaay, I'm stepping out of this conversation. You are on your own, Sis," and leaves shaking her hands as if air drying them after handwashing.

Nathan and I laugh. I pat him on the arm and move on. Aunt Wendy is looking at me with wonderment and love. I want to start crying all over again.

"Your dad showed me the pictures," She said. "There were two of them, each with a newspaper. Just so you know, they'll be forever on the internet. Your hair looked good." Aunt Wendy says, straight faced.

I look at her and she gives me this goofy look back. She knows I don't care about how my hair looks on a ransom photo. She is just saying the most absurd thing to keep me from crying. How does she know me so well?

Aunt Wendy continues, "I wish I would have been there to see you two in action when you took that Wallace creep down. That would have been something I would have paid to see. I saw the picture the police took of Wallace in the sleeping bag. We were worried sick. The demands went to your mom and dad, the college Foundation, and the police. It appears the Foundation does not pick up over the weekend. When the police finally found the coordinator, he went right into a closed session with the CCC lawyers. I guess we'll never know if they intended to help or not."

I hug Aunt Wendy and thank her for being there. I can feel my energy starting to wane. I look over to Rachel, who is holding hands with Dave, and I can see she is as exhausted as I am.

I look back and see Eric there. Always there making sure I'm safe. He comes forward and gives me a long hug.

"Hey, you stood me up," he signs, looking all hurt. "Good thing you escaped, I was going to have to sell my car to help with the ransom."

"Yes, that would have been about a half million," I roll my eyes knowing that his car is worth $1,500 on a good day. Still, a very nice gesture. "I know how you love your car."

I ask Eric if he knows anything about our car. I'm told that Aunt Wendy and Franz went to pick it up and will drive it to our house. We're going home with Mom and Dad who are probably not going to let us out of their sight.

Just when I think we can go home, in come reporters from Tandy and Portland papers. Rachel re-tells the story and they ask questions like, 'Were you scared?' and 'How do you feel now?' These questions are designed to tie everything together in a little bow. They are the most exhausting. Rachel looks at Dad who thanks the reporters for their interest but plans on taking his daughters home right now.

With that, we all move towards the doors, camera lights occasionally flashing.

Back home we shower, eat a big bowl of soup with buttery toast, and go to bed. I don't know how long we sleep, but Rachel is already up when I get up. I think it was 12-15 hours. I'm stiffer than I thought I'd be. The welts are still on my wrists; I wonder when they will go away.

When I go upstairs, there is Rachel digging into a bowl of cereal. She points to the Sunday paper mid-chew. We're being called heroes. I roll my eyes at my sister. The article includes what happened before with Eric and the school lockdown. It has pictures of the house where we were held and pictures showing how Wallace looked before and after he dyed his hair. The reporters do a pretty good job on our story, but some of the language was over the top: "brave beauties" "tenacious twins." Oh, brother.

The lights flash and I go to see who is ringing the doorbell. It is a messenger (on Sunday?) who starts talking to me. I touched my finger to my ear and shake my head. She hands over two envelopes, gives me a pen, and shows me where to sign for them, which I do.

Once the door is closed, I open my envelope and give a big "Yay."

I rush the other envelope in to Rachel. She sees an envelope with her name on it from the Chenoa Foundation. I nod my head yes and tell her to hurry and open it up. I can't stop jumping up and down.

She opens the envelope and reads:

"Dear Rachel Carn,

Because of your heroic efforts in keeping our Foundation safe, Chenoa Community College wishes to award you the remainder of your schooling tuition free. This includes Winter and Spring of this year and Fall, Winter, and Spring of the next up to 15 credits per term.

Please accept our sincerest appreciation,

Chenoa Community College Foundation Board"

WHAT? We cannot believe it. We do our happy dance around the kitchen table and then run to the living room to share the good news with Mom and Dad.

Chapter 26

The State of Oregon vs Wallace

The time limit for a speedy trial in Oregon from the charge to the first day in court is 90 days. Rachel and I are in the first month of our second term at Chenoa Community College. We're not concerned with confronting the kidnapper, but the idea of going through the entire trial and being questioned in court feels intimidating.

For the month of November, both Rachel and I have had nightmares of being bound and not being able to get to the other person in time. But after that the nightmares became less frequent. When we learn the trial date is to be the second week in January, we start having the nightmares again. We don't know if the reason we're having the same dream is because we're twins, or that we have experienced the kidnapping together.

Stacie Wallace, Steve's sister, has the charge 'accessory' added to her charges since she lied when she pretended to inform on her brother. Still, her crimes are much less than those of her brother. She takes a plea instead of going to trial. She is now spending four years in Oregon's Coffee Creek facilities in Wilsonville with the possibility of probation after the first 28 months. While she is an accessory to her brother's crimes and lied to the police, she did not commit any violence.

The trial starts January 14th. It is to last two days at the most. Mom and Dad, Aunt Wendy, Nathan, and Dave come along for moral support.

Steve Wallace is being charged for all the crimes his sister is guilty of, the embezzlement of half a million in Chenoa Foundation funds, but added to that is falsifying records to get the Security Guard job at the college. He paid an old pal of his to pretend to be the CEO of a big business. This way when the 'CEO' was contacted about Wallace, his buddy gave him a glowing review. It was easy to find the buddy and have him roll over on his 'old pal.'

The security company Chenoa uses to hire the guards gets a bit of a black eye when it is found that they are fooled into hiring someone with falsified records. Their HR has a lot of explaining to do. They promise double background checks on all guards in the future.

The main focus of the trial is the kidnappings. The state decides to charge Wallace with kidnapping each person which would be six charges instead of two.

The Head of the Chenoa Foundation is not required to attend, so gives an affidavit to the state lawyers. Rachel and I learn that Eric and Franz also received letters from the college thanking them for their assistance when they were kidnapped and left tied in the office. I shudder when I think of it. Thank goodness Franz was there to step through the zip-ties that held her wrists. And it was Eric's long arm that twisted through the broken glass to free the door.

The Foundation gave them each financial support for their education. We think it is Chenoa's way of saying…here's some money. Please don't sue us. Both Eric and Franz accepted the financial support.

Once the trial begins, Eric, Franz, Rachel, and I are seated behind the state prosecutor. I didn't particularly like everyone looking at us. Sara and Will, interpreters we know from Chenoa, are there as certified legal ASL interpreters. This means they are fully certified and have an additional training in legal interpreting.

Wallace sits beside his defense lawyer and doesn't even look back at us, which is a good thing.

On opening, the District Attorney lays out everything clearly point by point from the campus lockdown, to the kidnapping of the four of us in the Foundation Office at Chenoa, and then the kidnapping of my sister and myself, which includes the ransom demand.

Wallace's defense attorney's opening statement does not counter the charges, but explains how with the first kidnapping, the kids were in very little harm since he only threatened them to give himself time to get away. For the second kidnapping event, the lawyer emphasizes how he did not hurt us, he let us go to the bathroom when we needed and also brought us dinner and then breakfast. Obviously, the whole idea of Wallace's trial defense is to sway the jury as well as the judge, because Wallace is hoping for leniency because he never 'hurt' anyone.

Once the lawyers do their opening arguments, Eric is called to the stand to be sworn in. Eric first explains what happened in the Foundations office with Stacie Wallace, who he thought was the Foundation receptionist. He then goes on to identify Steve Wallace as the person who entered the office while Eric was being helped by Stacie. Eric also mentions that he identifies Wallace, days later, to the rest of his friends when he sees Steve Wallace approach the four standing outside the Foundation Office reading the sign. He identifies the person who pointed a gun in his face, took away his belongings, and stuffed him in a room zip-tied.

The defense lawyer counters asking Eric if he is sure that the man is really the Wallace sitting in court. The lawyer also hints that Wallace slipped the firecrackers into Eric's backpack, so he must not have been paying much attention.

Eric simply states that Mr. Wallace is the one he saw both times.

Next it is Franz's turn to get sworn in. They use her full name 'Francis,' and, if she was not so nervous, she would have winked at Aunt Wendy.

The DA asks if Franz can point out the man who approached her and her friends outside the CCC Foundation Center, lead them in, and then forced them to the back rooms with a gun. Franz nods and points to Wallace. The prosecutor thanks her.

The defense lawyer is not kind. He acts all confused. "Ms. Vega, you said that Mr. Wallace lead you into a room and then pulled a gun on you four. Why did you follow him into a room? Didn't your parents ever tell you about following strangers?"

Franz ignores his snide remarks and answers, "Wallace was wearing the uniform of a Chenoa Security guard and told us that he had some information to give us. Believe me...if he hadn't had that gun…"

If it had not been so serious, it would have been comical. The lawyer holding up his hand to silence Franz's signing while the interpreter keeps talking. Oh, lag time.

"That will be all," the defense says putting up his hand as to block her. "You are excused."

Next, my sister is sworn in. The interpreters re-position themselves to accommodate for the interpreting process. Rachel is sworn in and answers the questions about the events when she was the one who interpreted. She confirms the events described and states that she was the interpreter. She is thanked.

Wallace's attorney stands and asks my sister if maybe in all the confusion she interpreted incorrectly and the situation was not as dire as she made it seem?

I'm so proud of my sister. She looks the attorney right in the eye and says, "I'm fluent in English, Signed English, and ASL. I have been interpreting for my sister since we were two. I interpreted the spirit and intent of Wallace as clearly as any person can with a gun in her face."

Franz, Eric, and I do a low Deaf applause, and then put our

hands back in our laps.

She is excused.

Eric gives my hand a squeeze when I'm called. I'm sworn in last.

The DA goes through the same questions, and I point out Wallace. He then asks me why I called 911 when I saw Wallace approach.

I want my thinking to be clear, "I knew Eric was not the one who caused the hoax and the lockdown that started all this. When we were filling out our Foundation papers, we found that he had been given the wrong papers and given misinformation relating to signing the form. When he also told me the place was messy and that the woman had trouble finding things, I suspected something was wrong. Once we found the "closed" office sign, I started to create a hypothesis and called my sister and friend Franz. When Eric identified Wallace as the person in plain clothes who had been in the office, I was concerned, so texted 911 then slipped the phone in my backpack. I was hoping the police would come."

"Thank you, Ms. Carn," the State responds, "for your fine detective work."

The defense stands and says, "I know Wallace was carrying a gun, but did he harm you in any way? Hurt you? Wasn't he just giving himself a little time? It was not like he blindfolded you or gagged you, made you lay on the floor or anything."

If the attorney is trying to make it seem less threatening, he is asking the wrong woman. Instead of looking at the lawyer, I look at the jury. As soon as I do this the lawyer put up his hand and says. "That will be all, Ms. Carn."

I don't know why that makes me so mad. I know exactly what Wallace's strategy is. With the courage I didn't even know I had, I ask the judge if I could answer the question. This prompted the DA to ask the judge the same thing. The judge said that she would allow it.

I look at the jury and sign, "We were zip-tied with our hands in back. That is like being gagged for a Deaf person. Worse than gagged. It is like our tongues are removed, terrifying. As Wallace left, he turned off the lights. Since we were in a back office inside a larger office we were plunged in the worst darkness. So then he had our eyes. It was like being blindfolded and gagged and left for who knows how long. Some Deaf people also have balance problems and become dizzy and sick in total darkness. So it was harmful physically and emotionally. Very harmful."

With that, I leave the witness chair. I'll tell you, when I get back to my seat, I'm shaking like a leaf. I look over at the jury and one of the jurors gives me a tiny Deaf applause. That made my day. If Wallace thinks he can use us to make himself seem harmless, he has another thing coming.

It is time for Rachel to return to the stand. It is stipulated that she is already sworn in. The DA goes through the events as they occurred on the day she is kidnapped outside the college, including the note sent to her about the accident happening to her car. That paper and the notes had both been disposed of by Wallace in the house, so they were retrieved. They were put into evidence at that time.

Two pictures and a cell phone are then placed into evidence. Pictures of Rachel's friction burns and zip-tie welts are also put on the screen. I look over at Dave who is getting red in the face. I see his fists clench. I type in my cell, "It's okay, we've got him," and pass the cell over to Dave. He nods and takes some deep breaths.

Wallace's lawyer stands and begins listing all the things that Wallace did to make our lives easier while kidnapped. He asks if Wallace brought food and let us go to the bathroom when we needed to. "He also kept on the light and took off the zip-tie when you wanted to talk to your sister. Did he not?" The lawyer isn't stupid. He knows the comments I made about the darkness made the jury shudder. He is still trying to show Steve Wallace's 'softer side.'

But my sister isn't buying it. "No," she answers.

The lawyer had to think back about his question. "He didn't take the zip-tie off you so you could talk to your sister?"

My sister looked right at him and said, "No. He took off the zip-tie so I could INTERPRET for my sister, so I could tell my sister how clever he was and how he tricked me and kidnapped me. He picked up a pillow and told me that if I did not come back from the bathroom quickly enough he would use the pillow as a silencer and kill my sister while she was tied to chair, helpless."

The lawyer has his hand up and is saying, "That is all, Ms. Carn," but she just keeps right on talking until she is done.

"He wanted my hands because he wanted to make sure we were terrified. The only thing he did that really helped was when he brought us coffee so we could throw it in his smug face right before I hit him with a lamp and knocked him out cold." With that, she leaned back in her chair.

The lawyer sits and puts his head together with his client. Just as quickly, the lawyer pops up and asks to see the DA and the Judge in her chambers. We're all excused for a 30 minute recess.

"What do you think is going on?" I wonder.

Franz signs "I don't know for sure, but since Wallace is looking worse, not better in front of the jury, he might be trying to make a deal. If that is true, it could end today."

We go out to the halls, find a vending machine with any kind of coffee, and freshen up. We all gather together and are just lost in our own thoughts. I sit between Mom and Dad, because I don't want there to be any kind of drama between Nathan and Eric. After more than two months they are pretty good about ignoring each other while in the same room.

Nathan is taking his second term of American Sign Language, and using what he is learning with his little brother. Our biology study sessions have really paid off, as we challenge each other to keep up our grades. Eric is still walking that line between friendship and romance. It's a new year, a new term. Who knows what this year will bring. What mystery might be around the next corner?

We're called back after 30 minutes. Wallace and his lawyer are not there. The jury is thanked by the judge for doing their civic duty. They are excused since there is a settlement made. I look at Mom and

Dad; we all start signing at once.

The DA stands while the jury files out. He then turns and looks at the four of us, Rachel, Eric, Franz, and me, raises his hands, and gives us a Deaf applause.

Discussion Questions from the Author

This book is not only a mystery, it can be a way to learn about Deaf people, Deaf culture, and American Sign Language. The answers to the following questions (ones students asked me each term) are found throughout the book:

1. Is American Sign Language (ASL) universal?

2. What is a name sign?

3. What is the difference between ASL and signed English?

4. What is the Oral Method?

5. What is the difference between big "D" Deaf and little "d" deaf?

6. How do Deaf people "whisper?"

7. Is there a difference in how Deaf people hear?

8. What are some different ways people become Deaf?

9. What is DPN?

10. How did DPN impact the way Deaf people see themselves.

A Nod to Nancy Drew

There is a secret in this book. When I was younger, I was a great fan of the Nancy Drew Mystery Novels. I read every book I could collect. As a matter of fact, Nancy Drew saved my life.

When I first moved to Oregon from Kansas in my 20's I wanted to make sure I could find my way around Portland. This was before cell phones allowed us to carry a map everywhere we traveled. I would fill up my tank and get lost on purpose. I would drive this way and that for about 30 minutes. Once good and lost, I would find my way home. I learned a lot about the city, driving solo.

One day I went farther than usual. I was getting in some higher terrain and saw beautiful cityscapes. I noticed that I needed either to turn back or turn on to what was called a logging road. Oh nice, I innocently thought, a road that leads to a logging area. That would probably be a great view. Asphalt turned to gravel that was deeply sunk in. Okay, I told myself, time to turn around and get home. I did a three point turn, but on the last turn I could feel my back tires sink.

Oh, no… I was miles from…well, I didn't know where I was.

I got out and saw that, indeed my tires were sunk in gravely mud. I got back in and rocked the car which made it worse.

I yelled for a while and honked my horn until I felt foolish. No one was coming. I was without a blanket, water, or even matches. If I were to start walking now, I thought, it would take me too long to get to the last place I saw people. And they might be gone. Also it was getting dark and … bears. I felt discouraged, foolish, and was starting to be genuinely scared.

Suddenly I thought, "What would Nancy Drew do?" Frankly that idea popping in my head made me laugh out loud. Just laughing made me feel better. I mean, how many books had I read where Nancy Drew had gotten herself out of bigger problems than this? So, I put on my Nancy Drew persona and took a fresh look at my situation, walking slowly around the car.

I formulated a plan and got to work, filling the holes with rocks and sticks that I carefully gathered nearby. It would be like a driving off on a wooden raft. Pleased with my handiwork, I got into my car, started the engine and drove out of the sunken areas. I rolled down the windows and cheered as I drove down the mountain side, "Thank you, Nancy Drew!"

Indeed, Nancy Drew saved my life. In honor of all the books demonstrating girl power, I've given a tip of the hat to Nancy Drew hidden in my first book of fiction.

Here's a clue: Remember Aunt Wendy? Re-arrange the letters in the name, Wendy Carn. Enjoy the mystery.

About the Author

Bobbi Bowman spent more than 20 years as a sign language interpreter, teacher, and trainer. She has taught Deaf students English and hearing students American Sign Language. Bowman used this extensive background to infuse this mystery with information about American Sign Language and Deaf culture.

Bowman lives in Salem, Oregon with her family.

Additional Books by Bobbi Bowman

The Sailor and the Piano Teacher

Non-fiction, transcribed letters between two young people during WWII.

Goldfish Diaries

Collection of cartoons on the musings of a goldfish.

A Gift at the Door

Children's picture book

Bully Pie

Children's picture book

Upcoming Books by Bobbi Bowman

Bee Wars

Children's Picture Book

Finally Home

Children's Picture Book

Made in the USA
San Bernardino, CA
04 November 2019

59407455R00102